THE AMAZING HARRY HOUDINI

AIRSHIP 27 PRODUCTIONS

The Amazing Harry Houdini Volume 1

"Houdini Brings the Curtain Down" © 2015 Jim Beard
"Houdini and the Spear of Destiny" © 2015 James Palmer
"Houdini and the Catacombs of Paris" © 2015 I.A. Watson
"Magician's Razor" © 2015 Roman Leary

Published by Airship 27 Productions
www.airship27.com
www.airship27hangar.com

Interior illustrations © 2015 Pedro Crus
Cover illustration © 2015 Carl Yonder

Editor: Ron Fortier
Associate Editor: Gordon Dymowski
Marketing and Promotions Manager: Michael Vance
Production and design by Rob Davis

ISBN-13: 978-0692586563 (Airship 27)
ISBN-10: 0692586563

Printed in the United States of America

10 9 8 7 6 5 4 3 2 1

THE AMAZING HARRY HOUDINI

"HOUDINI BRINGS THE CURTAIN DOWN"

BY

JIM BEARD

She had been conversing with ghosts again.

But that, she recognized, was the least of her family's problems; why they chose to fixate on her comings and goings and ignore what was right under their noses was beyond her ability to comprehend. Now, things were bad. Maybe as bad as they'd ever been before.

The girl stepped swiftly down the bustling, busy street of her hometown without a distinct purpose in mind—no, strike that. She *did* have a purpose, a mission, though she didn't quite know the means to the end. Not yet. But something would happen and soon; she was sure of it. Hadn't the ghost told her that?

No, that just wouldn't do, her family had told the girl. Maybe that sort of thing passed muster a hundred, two-hundred or more years ago, but here, in the first few years of the twentieth-century, it just wouldn't do. Talking to spirits? No, no; not in *this* family, they told her. Fads of table-tappers and so-called mediums be damned.

The girl—a young woman, actually—would be expected to pull herself up from such childish things and draw upon her the cloak of civility and decorum which the family had woven and stitched carefully over several decades. She would take on the *responsibilities* of her heritage. And she would no longer talk to or talk of ghosts.

She stopped suddenly and looked, really *looked* around herself at her surroundings. London was once again drawn in misty lines and shadows from the light rain that had begun that morning and continued to fall well into the afternoon. The girl took in the throngs of people, all hurrying about their business like worker ants and taking no notice of her whatsoever. She had wondered if she looked a fright, but no, no one paid her any mind and so she continued headlong on her way down the swelling Strand.

5

What was she looking for? That is what she asked herself. *Help*. It was as simple as that. Help. Aid. A solution to war, to strife, to a situation that had escalated beyond reason and threatened her world and that of her family. The girl winced at the thought of what her relatives would say if she had told them what she was about—the disdain, the condescension on their faces loomed before her, real and palpable. She shook off the mental images and hurried on.

The girl turned to the north and made her way deeper into the city. The smells of cooking assailed her, mingled with the sweat of the citizens she passed and accentuated by the misty moisture that hung in the air. Despite it all, all the myriad sights and odors and actions around her, her mind wandered once again and soon her surrounding blurred into nebulous distractions.

Get help. Seek aid. Solve the problem of your family.

Then, as if in queer response to her plight, turning a corner and entering an open square she saw the man suspended in mid-air before her.

～♋～

Houdini had long felt that he did his best, most clear thinking while upside-down.

The young man in the impeccable evening dress flexed his muscles against the rough, white cloth of the straightjacket in which he was bound and rattled the chains which encircled him. Then, he looked at the crowd that had gathered below him on the street and he smiled. His presence-of-mind, his strong thoughts, lent him strength.

Harry Houdini was never more alive then when he was performing. The youthful magician had previously made a name for himself throughout the United States and had now embarked on a whirlwind assault on Europe, beginning in England. In a few short weeks, he had become the "Sensation of London" and his tour of the city now culminated in this most daring, most dangerous of wonders: a mid-air hanging escape. These Londoners loved him already, he mused, and he set about giving them a show they'd never forget.

Securely bound hand and foot and body, and hanging upside-down from a crane seven stories over Leicester Square, Houdini felt his mind becoming increasingly untroubled and free of mundane worries. He had only to free himself from his quite-secure restraints and, in doing so, survive the inevitable plunge to the street below that said freedom would bring.

Houdini was in his element.

He had thought perhaps the rain, a peculiar British variety of fine, chilled droplets, might vex him, but the moisture on his face served only to sharpen his senses. In a moment, Houdini would perform one of his greatest escapes and in full view of his audience. It would be a show-stopper if there were anything else to the show that could possibly follow it.

Below him, hundreds of faces looked up with varying expressions. The young magician gazed out at the teeming mass of Londoners, taking in people from all walks of life. There, before and below him, were laborers and businessmen, fishwives and governesses, and riders of horse-trams and horse-buses—all wondering to themselves as to who this strange young man might be and why he was hanging upside-down and disrupting their errands. Houdini also saw awe and fright on some of the normally-reserved British countenances.

Good, he thought. I have shaken them from their normal routine—now to amaze them.

He slipped his hands, still underneath the straightjacket, free from a pair of cast-iron manacles. The restraints were placed upon him by no less than a local magistrate and deemed secure by the worthy's own wife. Houdini, the famous "Handcuff King" of America, found them to be no barrier to his indomitable will to be free.

He then spotted a small gathering of reporters below on the street. One in particular, Houdini remembered, was from *The Daily Mail*, a punchier, popular newspaper from which the magician especially desired some good press. He nodded his head at the reporter. There was also a man from the *London Evening Sun*.

So, too, were there officers of the local police force.

Houdini sighed inwardly and shook his head. He and his manager had gone through the proper channels, as always, to insure his spectacles of magic were well within the guidelines of the law, but this time he had run into a bit more than the usual amount of resistance. That resistance came from a surly fellow named Sergeant Bolt. Potentially a good stage name for a magician, Houdini pondered.

Bolt had ranted and railed a bit, in a quiet sort of English manner, but, in the end, he acquiesced and allowed the young performer the permits he needed to stage his event. Another Houdini victory. He knew his stunts were not exactly commonplace and reeked of danger—that was what made them spectacles—but he was always careful to stay within the strictures of the law.

Enough reverie, he thought. Now to throw off the straightjacket and chains. He began to shift and compress his shoulders to allow his hands and fingers access to the edge of the cloth…

Then, suddenly, a voice from the building behind him broke Houdini's concentration.

⚙

"Harry, Harry," called the voice. "I am sorry to interrupt, but there is someone here who says they need urgently to speak to you."

Houdini swung his head around and, in doing so, managed to revolve in place to face the building. There, only a few feet from where he hung from the crane, the sheepish face of his manager Martin Beck looked out at him through a window.

"Martin, do you truly feel that this is the very *best* time to bring me such news?"

Beck's face, round and thick, twisted into a scowl. "Perhaps I am only making up a lie so as to bring you inside? To maybe save your life? What would happen to me if you perhaps killed yourself? I would be destitute, yes?"

Houdini smiled; it was his manager's old song and dance. "I shall be done here in only a minute or so, Martin. It can't wait?"

"She's very pretty," came the reply.

Houdini swiftly swung back around to face his audience, freed his hands from the straightjacket, released the chains that bound him, and doffed the jacket. It fell to the cobblestones below. The crowd cheered. Then, the magician reached up to release his ankles from their bindings and hung from the main chain while the crane deposited him through the window and back inside.

With one dramatic bow at the window, he acknowledged the city once more and then he and Beck hurried to his meeting.

⚙

Martin Beck glanced sideways at his client as the two men rode a lift to the hotel's lobby below. The portly Slovakian impresario gazed at the young man who stood at his side and once again marveled at the last few years of their partnership.

Houdini had met Beck in St. Paul, Minnesota and the young man's talent for showmanship and dynamic illusions impressed him to such a degree that he knew his future would be dominated by the performer. Now, here they were in London, England after having conquered the United States and Houdini was surely poised to enamor the entire world.

Beck sighed inwardly, though, at his young charge's penchant for "do-gooding." Bad enough that Houdini risked life and limb with his more outré stunts, but the magician also seemed to attract trouble like some sort of human magnet. Already, in the relatively short time they had been in London, Houdini had exposed a nest of criminals and cutthroats and had even rescued a clutch of orphans from a blazing asylum.

It will not be the escapes from seven stories up that will kill the Amazing Houdini, Beck mused; it will be his too-big heart.

～◯◯◯～

The elevator deposited the two men in the grand lobby of the hotel from which Houdini had both made his base and presented his hanging escape. Beck took a step forward to lead his charge to his impromptu meeting, but the magician surged ahead like a bloodhound on the scent. Beck sighed and simply followed.

Houdini trod briskly through the busy lobby and then paused to take in his surroundings. Almost at once, he seemed to spot his quarry and stepped in that direction. He halted in front of a girl who occupied one of the opulent chairs that dotted the space.

"Err, may I present to you," stuttered Beck to the girl in his thick accent, out of breath from catching up. "Mister—"

"I am Houdini," interrupted the performer, who bowed deeply and smiled. He held out one hand, open palm up.

The girl rose out of her chair to take the proffered hand. Houdini saw immediately that she was hardly a girl, but not yet quite a woman. He guessed her to be nineteen or so. He was also immediately intrigued.

Before him she stood, dressed in a simple frock of good cotton. Nothing ostentatious, but the girl wore it well. Houdini admired her pleasing figure and the lustrous midnight black hair that fell about her shoulders, framing a round face with eyes almost as dark as her hair, a somewhat-aquiline nose and full, well-shaped lips. The magician found himself staring intently into those deep, almost-black eyes. The mesmerist was himself mesmerized.

"Mister Houdini," she said with a full, clear voice. "Thank you so much for seeing me."

Houdini smiled the more. "Well, now that I have seen you—how may I help you?"

He motioned for her to sit again and he pulled up another chair to position himself close to her, but keeping a decorous distance.

"My name is Rose Mannfred," she began, looking Houdini squarely in the eye. "My family owns the Lyceum Theatre, on Wellington Street…"

With this, Houdini glanced over at Beck, a questioning look on his face. His manager raised an eyebrow and executed a curt shake of his head and a slight shrug of his shoulders.

"…and we are in desperate trouble."

～ↄ¤ᴄ～

Rose Mannfred noticed the silent exchange between the two men. Her eyes darted back and forth between them, demanding their attention.

"It is not widely known that the Mannfreds own the property, but we have for many, many years. Often to our chagrin and heartache, I'm afraid. But, of late, we have fallen into dire circumstances!"

Houdini, realizing he had been leaning towards Rose and worked himself into an indelicate position, straightened himself and looked at her with piercing eyes. "Please, what can you tell me of these troubles?" he said.

"Oh, Mister Houdini, I'm not sure where to begin—if my family knew I was coming to you, they, well, they would be furious. But, they've blinded themselves to what is happening and I fear for their safety…and that of our beloved Lyceum.

"You see, the theatre has a history of troubles, some of a quite violent nature. It has been saddled with a kind of, well, *civil war*, I guess you could say. There are two sides to our family, if you will. And they are tearing each other apart."

Houdini affixed a polite smile to his face. "My dear Miss Mannfred, I appreciate that you think so highly of me to approach me with your tale, but, honestly, and I do apologize, I am not exactly in the rude habit of inserting myself into the middle of family squabbles."

"No, no!" flared the girl, her black eyes lit with anger. "You don't understand! No one understands but me! Why must I be saddled—wait, please." She tried to compose herself. "If you come to the Lyceum and see for yourself, perhaps then it will be clear. Perhaps we can arrange for you to, to…perform there?"

Beck interjected himself at this juncture. "Do you speak for the owners on this sort of matter, miss? Do you have the authority to offer Mister Houdini this proposition?"

Rose dropped her chin to her chest. Her entire carriage changed, from proud young woman to resigned, frightened girl. Houdini was amazed at the forces that ran through her frame, animating her one moment, fleeing from her the next. With eyes that missed nothing, that sought truth and filtered out falsehood, he witnessed her inner turmoil.

"No, I don't suppose I do," she sobbed quietly. "But you *will* come."

Houdini then found himself in the unenviable position of staring down the barrel of a pistol.

⌐꧁꧂⌐

Beck gasped, fell backwards, his hands flying up and rotating in shock. Houdini remained calm. He leaned forward a bit, towards the girl.

"Miss Mannfred," he said slowly. "What is your full Christian name?"

The girl blinked in surprise, but the gun stayed in place, aimed at the magician's heart. A tear fell from the corner of one eye into her lap.

"Ros-Rosalina..." she stuttered. The tremor then extended to the hand that grasped the small pistol.

Houdini smiled. "A very pretty name. I thought perhaps it was something even more exotic than 'Rose.' I would like to talk with you further on your proposition, Rosalina, but I am afraid for these poor people," - he gestured widely to the lobby's inhabitants—"and do not wish to alarm them with gunplay. You agree?"

The girl's eyes followed Houdini's hand. His movements were smooth and practiced, like Delsarte, and strangely hypnotic. The magician then slipped an embroidered handkerchief from one cuff of his jacket and raised it to his brow, as if to wipe away a bead of perspiration.

"Of-of course..."

"Oh, I am so very glad," enthused Houdini. And then he flicked the handkerchief with a broad flourish toward Rose. It settled over the pistol.

Before the girl had realized what had happened, the magician whisked the cloth away and with it her weapon. She stared dumbly at her empty hand. Then, she collapsed into the chair, bent over her lap and wept.

Houdini leaned forward the more and touched Rose lightly on the shoulder in a reassuring manner. With his other hand he slipped the pistol from his pocket and held it out gingerly to his manager. His eyes never left the sobbing form of the girl.

"Well, Martin," he said, barely above a whisper. "It seems we will be making a trip to the famous Lyceum Theatre after all…"

◦⟳◦

Several minutes later, Houdini, Beck and Rose stepped into a Hansom cab outside the hotel and were on their way.

Certain persons in the crowd on Leicester Square watched the departure. Then, they turned to each other. After a moment of silence, one of the men spoke.

"An unexpected development. *He* won't like it."

"No," said another. "That's why we'll have to do something about it."

◦⟳◦

It hadn't dawned on Houdini that he had become quite distracted by Rose Mannfred until the wooden cane impacted against the side of his head, sending him sprawling backwards into the side of the hansom. By that point, it was painfully obvious.

The magician rubbed his jaw and looked up at his attacker, remembering that the girl had said little more on the ride to the Lyceum, save that the venerable theatre was in poor financial straights and caught in the middle of a kind of power struggle.

Houdini wondered if this new wrinkle had anything to do with said struggle.

Only a few scant seconds had passed after he, Rose and Beck had pulled up to the entrance of the Lyceum on Wellington when a broad, swarthy face appeared at the window of the cab, ordering them out of the conveyance in a rough, heavily-accented voice.

"Stay in the cab," said Houdini to Beck and Rose, curtly. He then exited to find himself face-to-face with a ruffian.

The man was dressed in many layers of somber clothes and wore a dirty cap atop his scraggly head. His face held a look of contempt, despite his obvious low-bearing; he sneered at the young performer as king would to a scullery-boy.

"May I help you, my good man?" was all Houdini managed to get out before a vicious blow from the man sent a spike of pain through his head. Inside the cab, he heard Beck squeak in surprise and the girl protest the rough treatment. Recovering, Houdini reassessed his opponent.

The thug had produced what at first the performer saw as stick or a baton, but what he now discerned as a kind of cane. Wooden and sturdy, it was crooked at one end, its length was no more than that of a man's arm. Its wielder held it out like a fencing foil, his thumb set along its shaft, and waggled it at Houdini.

Houdini raised his fists and turned his body to provide less of a target for the man, but in a blur of motion the ruffian darted in and cracked the stick soundly against his shoulder. The pain was instant and pronounced.

The magician jabbed savagely at the man, landing a blow on his razor-free chin. Houdini bounced back, glad to have gotten in a solid hit, but his opponent wasted no time in delivering a counter-attack. He came at the young man like a jousting knight.

The stick whistled past Houdini's head. He counted himself lucky that time, but the thug deftly flicked his wrist and drove the cane against the back of Houdini's skull. It connected with a loud crack, sending the magician to his knees, stars dancing before his eyes.

Then came a withering series of lightning blows. Houdini staggered, nearly dropping completely to the ground. But he had already weathered many tortures in his young life and took the blows bravely until he could regain his senses. In a way, the sharp pains of the attack brought him some needed clarity.

He stood up abruptly and from his hand a bright flare of light sprang out before the eyes of the ruffian. The man grunted and grabbed at his face.

Houdini moved in with his fists. One, two, three; his blows rained down on his opponent, sending him wobbling backwards against a column. The stick drooped in the man's grimy hand, but then snapped back into pointed attention.

"What about me?" came a sudden voice from behind the man. He wheeled his head around, wary of another adversary, but inexplicably found no one there. Houdini pressed the advantage he'd gained from his ventriloquism and drove one fist into the thug's stomach and then another to his jaw. Stumbling backwards, his opponent dropped the stick and pitched his bulk into the wall of the theatre with a meaty thud.

Houdini leapt forward like a hare. A glint of cold steel flashed in the air and before it could register on his senses, the ruffian found his wrist encircled by one half of a pair of handcuffs, the other half around a pipe running up the side of the building.

The magician stooped to pick up the man's stick and then quite pointedly broke it over his knee.

Beck stepped from the hansom in time to hear his young charge say something to the thug in another language than English. Behind him, Rose flew from the cab and raced to Houdini's side.

Police whistles rent the air. Beck hurriedly closed the gap between himself and Houdini, eager to hear any sort of explanation for the attack before the local constabulary arrived. They had had more than a few moments of contact with the law in their years together, he and the young magician, and knew just how Houdini comported himself around badges and bluecoats. That is to say, he didn't much favor them.

"Are you hurt?" Beck heard Rose ask Houdini. He could see the concern on her face and frowned to himself. Females and trouble; a dangerous mixture where the magician was concerned.

Houdini mildly dusted himself off, readjusting his clothes as if he had only encountered the merest of inconveniences. "Only a bit worse for wear, my dear. Though I do wonder what this fellow was on about."

Beck looked down the street to see if he could spot the oncoming police. He turned back to Houdini. "What did you say to him, Harry? Did I hear you speaking—"

"Italian, yes," replied the magician, a grim smile on his lips. "I recognized the fighting style, a kind of martial stick art. An Italian variety. Very fascinating to see it used in such a setting. But I felt very strongly that I needed to tell my friend here, in his own language, that his stance was sloppy and his sportsmanship woefully lacking."

"My-my family, half of them that is, is Italian…" said the girl, quietly, wide-eyed. She then looked plaintively at Houdini. "Oh, no. No, it…oh, sweet lord. It's happening again."

"What the devil is going on here, Rose?" boomed a voice from the Lyceum's entrance. All three looked up to see an imposing figure of a man striding towards them, a scowl etched into every pore of his face and two young nasty-looking chaps trailing.

⌐ꝜꞘꞇ

For the second time in mere minutes, Houdini was forced to endure a homely face in rather too close a proximity to his own. But it did not belong to the tall man who exited the Lyceum, but rather hung ungainly from the head of one Sergeant Bolt, of the London Police Department.

Built like a fireplug and bullet-headed, the good sergeant steamed into Houdini's field of vision, fiery of face and demeanor.

The magician quite pointedly broke it over his knee.

"What do you mean by holding this man here?" he bellowed, pointing at the handcuffed ruffian. "You've no right, as a civilian, to incarcerate anyone—and I've no crumb of concern for who you are, sir!"

"Then I have nothing really to say, Sergeant," said the magician, biting back a more sarcastic retort. He held up a hand to cut his manager off from interfering. "Except that this person waylaid myself, Mister Beck here and Miss Rose Mannfred..."

"As I approached the scene, I saw only *you* attacking this man, sir. *And* breaking his property. You'll let this fellow go this very second, sir!"

Houdini just then spied another policeman, evidently a higher-ranking officer by his uniform, speaking to the men from the Lyceum. "My uncle and my cousins," whispered Rose from behind him. Without taking his eyes off the duo, he replied to Bolt.

"Let him escape on his own, Sergeant. I do it frequently myself—it's quite easy."

Rose's uncle, a tall man with expensive clothes, a clean-shaven face and slitted, bored eyes, broke his conversation with the other officer and sidled over to the young performer. The bulldog-like Bolt opened his mouth to further denounce Houdini, but his presence was then requested by his superior with a curt jerk of the man's head.

"I am Sir Roger Mannfred, owner and proprietor of the Lyceum," said the tall man. He did not extend his hand. "And you are, sir?"

"Uncle Roger," began Rose. "This is Mister—"

"I am Houdini."

Mannfred's eyes sparked a bit, but the dint of interest faded as quickly as it appeared and he narrowed his gaze once again in a disapproving sort of fashion.

"Ah, the renowned prestidigitator." He made it sound as if it were something to be ashamed of. He swiveled his head to take in his niece. "Rose, I overheard what you said to this man. I will not have you speaking of personal family matters to complete strangers. I will not have it."

Houdini raised a hand. "Please do not chastise the young woman, sir. It was *I* who, err, pressed *her* for information on the theatre and its history—I am to understand that the establishment is encountering difficulties? I have had some small experience with theatres and—"

Mannfred leaned slightly towards the young magician. He lowered his voice and looked Houdini straight in the eye.

"The Lyceum Theatre is a jewel of this fair city. It has stood for decades, weathering fires and other sorts of disasters, both on and off its stage. My family has seen it through thick and thin. The day that we should require the aid of such as yourself is the day that I allow it to crumble into dust.

"Am I clear on that point, sir?"

"Crystal," said Houdini, simply. He did not blink nor lower his own gaze. The two men held the pose for long seconds, silently, until Rose spoke up again, demanding Mannfred's attention.

"Uncle," she said, taking the magician's arm. "Mister Houdini is my guest. I intend to show him around the place. He shall be my responsibility. I hope you won't mind?"

"If you must," replied her uncle, and with that he spun on his heel and stalked back into the theatre, his glowering sons in tow.

"With all due respect, Miss Mannfred, I should like to meet your uncle in an alleyway somewhere."

Rose's midnight eyes appraised Houdini. "I'm afraid you'll have to get in line," she remarked grimly. "I love my uncle—he raised me after my parents died—but he's a large part of the problem. Now, if you and Mister Beck would follow me..?"

The trio took a few steps, but Houdini pulled up short and stopped. He suddenly realized he'd stood in the shadow of the theatre for many minutes now, but hadn't really *looked* at it. His eyes took in the Lyceum's magnificent set of columns and its peaked roof, its grandeur and stately presence. Still, too, he noticed age creeping in to the venerable structure and the unlit electrical sign that rested atop the building. Houdini felt he was looking at a dowager, a once-proud lady of means whose better days were fading into the past and with an uncertain future pressing down upon her.

"She was once the toast of London. 'Er stage boasted the cream of the theatrical crop, 'er seats the elite of society—and the common man, too. And 'er music came from around the world..."

The magician turned to face the source of the unexpected commentary. His gaze fell upon the other police officer on the scene.

He introduced himself as Chief Nelly and he smoothed down his rather large, bushy brown moustache with one hand while extending his other to Houdini. The young man took the hand and offered the niceties of a first greeting in return.

The chief, the head of the local police precinct, apologized for his man Bolt and assured Houdini there'd be no more lip from the sergeant. They would haul off the street thug, of course, and introduce him to a jail cell right quickly. And could Mister Houdini, at his convenience, please swing by the precinct to make a statement as to the attack?

"Probably just one of the local wastrels who 'aunt the streets, looking for an easy mark—err, beggin' your pardon, Mister Houdini," commented Chief Nelly with a somewhat dandified air, despite his apparent East End accent.

"Count me as one of your admirers, sir. You 'ave the entire London force in quite a tizzy—they're 'anging on every word of your daring escapes from 'andcuffs an' the likes. Some would like to lock you up permanently. More power to you, I say."

Houdini bowed to the policeman and made polite noises of appreciation. Internally, though, he wanted only to move along and tour the Lyceum—with Rose at his side, of course. He bid a warm farewell and a good day to the officer, promising to appear at the precinct as soon as possible.

Martin Beck, for his part, knew all too well what had happened to his star performer; he saw it emanating from every bone in Houdini's body. The Handcuff King had his teeth in it, a mystery and an enigma that demanded a solution. It was hid life's work, divining the magic around him and wrestling it into submission.

"I haven't even told you about the ghost yet," announced Rose, once again taking the magician's arm and steering him towards the waiting theatre doors.

Beck sighed, gritted his teeth and dutifully followed.

～ɔჟ૯～

A certain two gentlemen watched as Houdini entered the Lyceum. Without turning to the other, one of them spoke after observing in silence.

"I should have been notified of this sooner," he said in a dull voice. "This *person* should never have gotten as far as the threshold. He should never have stepped out onto the curb...or even taken the cab ride in the first place."

"It would never have occurred to me that our man would fail," implored the other.

The first man ignored his compatriot's whining and gazed up at the grand façade of the once-worthy theatre.

"Advance the timetable. Make it tonight. And make it forever."

～ɔჟ૯～

Sitting alone in the darkness, Houdini tried vainly to gather his thoughts, pondering the strange events of the day while looking out upon the great stage of the famous Lyceum Theatre.

After a splendid tour of the building with Rose—shadowed almost constantly by her glowering male cousins—he and his manager retired to their hotel where the magician ate an abbreviated meal, applied liniment to his bruises, changed into a more comfortable, but still fashionable suit and returned to the Lyceum. He had earlier proposed to Rose that he would stake out a spot in the seats after dark and lie in wait for her ghost—and delve to the bottom of the mystery.

Houdini, of course, had no real intention of ghost hunting at midnight in one of the world's most famous theatres, but it played well with the young woman and it allowed him access to the building. There, alone, he might discover the source of the problems Rose outlined and, perhaps, bring them to a conclusion.

The performer truly hated to misguide the girl, but a little white lie for a greater good he deemed a necessary evil.

The silence and darkness of the Lyceum assailed him. He marveled at the absence of sound in the old girl, an unlikely circumstance in such a venerable structure. His eyes soon adjusted to the dark and he gazed out at the stage, a sudden urge to tread its boards, performing his illusions and spectacles, racing through him.

There, on the stage—he could see it now, a kind of play. The story of a family, twisted apart by…jealousy? Anger? Those were the usual emotions that tore other such families asunder; why not the Mannfreds and the—what was the name of the other half of the family? Houdini realized he did not now, save that they were, allegedly, of Italian lineage. British and Italian. Not necessarily a volatile mix, but…anything was possible, he supposed.

The magician, in his mind's eye, conjured up Henry Irving, Britain's greatest living actor, taking the stage in the role of Rose's father…or perhaps even as Sergeant Bolt. What a lark that would be. And Rose? A role to be assayed by the beautiful Ellen Terry, the celebrated actress, of course. No one else could do Miss Mannfred justice.

Would there be a ghost? Surely. A sepulchral figure to rise up through a hidden trapdoor and intone cryptic nonsense…he nodded knowingly to himself. Houdini had faked a few spirits in his time, feeling certain he could spot any such attempts at moribund mummery should they present themselves in the course of his investigation.

Then, astoundingly, and as if in direct response to the young man's musings, a ghostly figure presented itself on the stage before his very eyes.

⁓꙳⁓

Most amazing, thought Houdini. He immediately assumed he'd entered into a sort of hypnogogic state, not fully allowing for how tired he was and imagining a spirit form gliding across the stage.

But it *did* glide. And it really *was* there. And it made no sound that his keen ears could discern.

The magician all but leapt out of his seat and rushed headlong down the row he occupied and into the aisle at its end. Trying to remain quiet and move as swiftly as possible, Houdini all but flew toward the stage and made a mighty leap from the orchestra pit to the edge of its boards. He crouched there upon landing, straining his senses to track the shadowy figure.

Houdini resisted the urge to pinch himself to insure that he was indeed not asleep.

There! he thought. *There you are, oh spirit!* Making great, long strides he rushed towards the curtains behind which the form had just disappeared. Reaching them, he grabbed at the long swaths of heavy material and whipped them to one side.

A man was revealed behind the curtain, frozen in mid-step, his face caught in a look of utter surprise.

"Who the devil are you?" demanded Houdini.

"Who am *I*?" replied the man, his voice laced with an Irish brogue. "Good Lord, sir—who are *you*? And what are you doing in my theatre?"

The magician reached out for the lapels of the man's coat and, having grasped them firmly, pulled the person into the faint light cast by a small electrical bulb that burned over an exit door nearby. The man grunted, taken by surprise by the seeming attack, and batted violently at Houdini's hands.

In the wan illumination, Houdini saw a portly man, in somber clothes of good quality and sporting a bristling beard of reddish hair. Wide, grey eyes opened and closed in disbelief above a ruddy face; the magician could see the anger building within the gentleman's countenance.

"What do you mean by this, sir? I am the manager of this theatre and I insist you identify yourself immediately - or I-I shall be forced to summon a policeman!"

"No, no, my friend," said Houdini, letting go the man's coat. "I have spoken to quite enough policemen for one day. I won't give you any more trouble.

"I am Houdini, and I am at your service, sir."

"HOUDINI?" said the man. "Surely, it can't—but yes, yes I can see that is…"

"And you, sir? You are…?"

The stout-figured man brushed down his coat and straightened it. "Stoker. Abraham Stoker, the manager of the Lyceum. Well, at least for the time being."

He held out his hand and the magician took it, shook it firmly.

"I apologize for the rough treatment, Mr. Stoker, most sincerely. But you gave me a bit of a start and…may I ask what you mean by 'for the time being'?"

Stoker looked as if his head was swimming and he swayed a little on the spot. "Ah, that's a story, but, Mr. Houdini, please; perhaps we should sit down and, ah, sort this all out? And, please call me Bram."

"Certainly," replied the young man with a smile. "You may call me… Houdini."

⁓ᘒᓂᓂᐣ⁓

"You say that Rose Mannfred asked you to…look into the theatre's business?" queried Stoker, after they had settled into a pair of seats not far from where the magician had been sitting. "I find that odd, if you don't mind my saying so."

Houdini nodded. "I agree it's a touch unorthodox, but the young woman is very distraught. When she came to me and asked for my help, well, I…"

"Yes, I see," said Stoker, averting his eyes, his ruddy cheeks reddening the more.

"What can you tell me of her family? Rose says there's a kind of struggle going on here at the Lyceum? She makes it sound for all the world like a matter of life and death."

The manager leaned forward a bit and clasped his hands together. After a moment, he looked up at Houdini with somewhat sheepish eyes.

"I'm terribly sorry, Mr. Houdini, but I'm not at liberty to discuss the personal business of my employers. Its not general public information that the Mannfreds own the Lyceum—"

"That's exactly what Rose said," interjected the magician.

"—but they have owned it for more than seventy years now. And had their share of ups and downs with it, like any business owners. Rose Mannfred is a…dreamer. Her parents died tragically when she was only four years old and…I'm sorry, but I overstep my bounds. Again, I cannot speak of it. It's not my place, you understand."

Houdini sighed, realizing he'd get nowhere with the man on that score. He recognized a bullish attitude when he saw one; he himself had cultivated his own. But how was he expected to help anyone if he could not glean the exact parameters of the problem?

He tried another avenue of exploration.

"I see that the Lyceum is preparing for another production—I am a huge fan of the theatre. Perhaps I should like to attend it. Which is it to be?"

A hint of sadness swelled behind Stoker's eyes. "We open with *The Merchant of Venice* in one week," he said, trying to sound prideful, but betrayed by his somber delivery. "It-it may be the final production of the Lyceum Theatre."

"Which explains your comment about being the manager 'for the time being'," Houdini replied sympathetically. "Business is bad, then?"

A tongue of fire sprang up then in the portly man's gaze. He fixed Houdini with a look of steely defiance.

"I *cannot discuss it*. I have already told you that, sir."

"Strange for you to be here so late at night, Mr. Stoker…"

The fire in Stoker's eyes flared up again. "I am the *manager* of this theatre, *sir*. I conduct my business how and when I see fit." He stood up. "This conversation is over. I shall see you to the door."

"But," noted Houdini, "without any lights burning? In the pitch dark?"

Stoker's resolve wavered a bit—the magician could see it immediately. He was most definitely nervous about something.

"Let me tell you something, Mr. Houdini, though it be against my better judgment. This theatre—" He gestured at their surroundings. "—has been plagued by fires and calamities for decades. Five years ago we lost almost our entire storage of sets and costumes to a fire. One unfortunate person actually lost their life to a blaze not long before I came to work here.

"It is my *duty*, my *obligation*, to see to the protection of the Lyceum. Do you understand that?"

Houdini heard the man's words and understood their meaning, but some part of his brain's workings, almost an unconscious part, sensed something else.

Perhaps it was all the talk of fires that began to influence the performer's train of thought, but he could have sworn that he smelled smoke just then.

"Hold a moment," he said to Stoker, raising a hand to reinforce his words. He swiveled his head around, taking in the theatre with his eyes and flaring his nostrils.

Suddenly, he looked back at the portly manager with alarm written across his face.

"Fire!"

Stoker moved at a speed that belied his girth; Houdini himself was hard-pressed to keep up with the Lyceum's manager. The magician saw the man take flight down the main aisle of the theatre and then along the edge of the stage to a door that stood off to one side. Faint wisps of smoke floated out from the open doorway.

Plunging through and into the room beyond, Stoker disappeared. Houdini, only a moment behind him, could hear voices from up ahead, in the other room. He could swear they were speaking Italian.

The manager's rich Irish brogue boomed out then, directed at whoever it was he had just seen, presumably. More yelling ensued.

Houdini dashed through the door and found himself in a small anteroom. It appeared to be a private rest area, a quiet chamber in which theatre patrons could wait during intermissions or even before a production began. It contained one long settee which stretched out along one wall and two chairs across from it, each occupying a corner.

The settee was on fire.

Smoke had begun to fill the small room, despite the fact that the blaze was not yet extensive. Houdini saw that the only other way out of the room was a much larger entranceway on the opposite side of the chamber, which did not have a proper door, but was filled by a large decorative column and a curtain which was hung across the opening. The magician saw the curtain swinging in place; obviously Stoker has just moved through it.

Thinking quickly, a trait prized by stage performers, Houdini doubled back and slammed shut the door he'd just come through. Perhaps it would serve to keep the fire from spreading out and into the theatre itself, he mused. Then, he turned to follow Stoker.

Taking a step toward the curtain, he pulled up short to see a tongue of fire leap from the settee to the large swash of heavy fabric. It caught there and ignited the curtain.

~ↃᗝᏏᏋᢁᘛᕀↄ~

Stoker ran after the arsonists with fury coursing through his veins. He thought of nothing save apprehending the interlopers, or at least identifying them for the police. He yelled out for them to stop, but they were already too wretchedly far ahead of him.

Slowing down, resignedly, two thoughts suddenly occurred to him: the fire, for one. And Houdini for another.

He wheeled about and dashed back towards the sitting room. Stoker called out to the magician.

"Don't shut that door! Don't—"

He heard the door slam closed.

"—shut the door."

Knowing full well that the door would lock upon closing and that he had left its key in his message box backstage, Stoker moved to pull Houdini from the small chamber.

Before he could re-enter the room, the privacy curtain was swiftly engulfed in flames. The magician was most likely trapped.

There was no way out, thought Stoker, panic gripping his heart and blood pounding in his head. The poor devil! The fire was filling the only way out, and the column, of course, but that only left a space between the decorative architectural feature and the edge of the doorway that roughly measured just six or seven inches...

Then, Stoker witnessed the most astounding sight.

The magician's face appeared in the gap between the column and the wall, then his hand, snaking its way through the opening and feeling around the column's smooth circumference. Stoker wanted to shout that it wasn't enough space to squeeze through...not enough space...the fire, the fire...oh, the humanity...

But then the theatre manager watched as Houdini, defying physics, seemed to ooze through the gap. The man's face wore a look of deadly earnest, of singular concentration as he did so. Stoker wanted to rub his eyes, wanted to disbelieve what they were communicating to his brain.

Houdini contorted himself, bit by bit, inch by inch, through a space barely wide enough to fit one arm through, let alone an entire body and attached head. It was an alien sight.

Within a matter of seconds, the magician was through the gauntlet and dusting off his suit. But he was not smiling.

❦

Houdini drew in a precious breath, then let it out. The smoke had made his eyes water and his breathing ragged. He felt across his arms and chest, and then rotated his neck. He felt dizzy. His vision blurred.

Someone was speaking. Were they speaking to him?

He felt heat at his back, then looked up to see Stoker before him. The man was speaking to someone. At first, Houdini thought it was Rose. Then, he realized with a start that it wasn't.

Houdini thought perhaps he was seeing a ghost.

"Do you believe in the supernatural, Mr. Houdini?"

The magician looked into the eyes of the speaker, questing for answers to his own wonderings, but found little of value there. Singed and bedraggled, Houdini found himself frustrated on many levels as he stood in the grand lobby of the Lyceum.

"I want to believe, Mr. Stoker," he told the theatre's manager. "But have found no real evidence of it. So, until such time that I do, I shall remain an enthusiastic skeptic."

"But-but, surely, in light of the incredible feats you have performed, including the quite astounding one I witnessed myself here tonight, you—"

Houdini held up a hand to interject; he had had this conversation many times before. "Life is full of mystery and illusion, sir, but the truth of the matter is that it is more often the latter than the former that we encounter. I stand on my previous statement. I cannot yet believe I saw a ghost tonight."

The fire that had threatened to block Houdini's way was thankfully confined to the small anteroom from which he escaped, and so easily doused by the few theatre employees who were in the vicinity. It became one more layer into which the magician felt he must dig to illuminate the vexing problem of the Lyceum's seemingly accursed status.

Suddenly, Rose Mannfred was at Houdini's side, placing a petite hand on his arm for attention. He guessed that the family maintained apartments somewhere on or adjacent to the property, as the young woman was dressed in evening gown and slippers.

"Its true, Mr. Houdini," she said. "The ghost of the Lyceum is very real. I have seen her—and talked with her."

Houdini looked to Stoker and then back again to Rose. "'Her'?" he asked.

Rose's eyes saddened. "Yes; it's a girl. She's very distraught. It was she that led me to *you*, for she told me that worse times were ahead for us if I didn't seek help…"

"Which," announced Houdini, wanting desperately to get to the heart of the matter. "Brings us to the very real problem of these men, these arsonists—Stoker, I distinctively heard them speaking Italian, like my attacker earlier. As far as I know, Italy is not at war with Britain, or America for that matter. What do you make of it?"

The russet-haired man blushed somewhat, stammering out a reply. "Well, I…I do believe I recognized them,"—he glanced sheepishly at Rose—"as, err, relations of the, ah, Mannfreds. But, I simply do not understand—"

Just then, a loud, booming voice interrupted Stoker. Houdini whirled around to see the stampeding advance of Rose's uncle, tying the sash of his robe tight and smoothing down a lock of errant hair. He looked to be quite furious.

"Stoker! What in the bloody hell's the meaning of all this?"

Rose Mannfred, stoking the coals of her own anger, attempted to defuse her uncle's ire, but to no avail; the theatre's owner was on a tear and nothing was to stand in the way of its execution.

"Good God!" pronounced Roger Mannfred, after hearing his manager's report of the intruders and their aborted arson. "Damn them all, anyway! That's it—the whole lot of them are dismissed! Immediately! Do you hear me, Stoker?"

"Every one of…" began Stoker. "You don't mean…?"

"Blast it all, man—*yes*! I want the entire band of rogues and assassins out this very moment!"

"Uncle Roger!" shouted Rose. "You can't really mean that—you are angry, surely, but you cannot put *family* out on the streets!"

Houdini tensed, ready to spring to the girl's defense, for he was certain just then that the man was about to strike his own niece. There would be none of that, the magician told himself, not while he continued to draw a breath.

Roger Mannfred clenched his jaw, gained some small control over his fury and then turned to Stoker once more.

"*Now*, Mr. Stoker. Right this very moment."

But before Houdini could wonder any further as to the precise parameters of the deep, yawning division in Rose's family, the universe, in its wide wisdom, dealt the young man a new hand, full of fresh pitfalls and problems.

"Stoker! What in the bloody hell's the meaning of all this?"

The London police, in the form of Sgt. Bolt and a few deputies, entered the building and made a bee-line straight for Houdini.

〜𝓞𝓞𝓒〜

Sitting in a Bow Street jail cell, Houdini found he had little time for reverie. The steady stream of players and acts on his mind's eye's stage was enough to keep him well-occupied.

Firstly, there was Bolt, who brazenly accused him of setting the Lyceum fire. The *basso profundo* officer of the law claimed he'd been given information that Houdini was responsible for the blaze and that he had the authority to take the magician into custody. Surprisingly, only Rose Mannfred objected. No one else at the theatre, most pointedly manager Stoker and owner Mannfred, raised their voice to speak to Houdini's innocence.

Secondly, the kind face of Chief Nelly appeared at the bars to the young man's cell to offer his abject apologies and assure Houdini that he'd be kept only as long as needed to sort through the "sad events," and then he'd be released on his own recognizance.

"I'm sorry," said Bolt's boss. "But there's nothing t'be done for it, I'm afraid…"

Thirdly, there were the many Bobbies and detectives who wandered in and out of the Bow Street station to get a look at the famous performer. The precinct's own officers were already fairly incensed at Houdini, as the magician had insisted on slipping off every single pair of handcuffs that could be placed upon him, from the time of his "capture" at the Lyceum and all the way through his transportation to his cell. It won Houdini few new admirers.

Then came Martin Beck. Houdini's own agent waddled into the station with a look on his round face the likes of which the magician had seen many times, a kind of glowering-depressive feature that spoke to Beck's mood at being rung up in the middle of the night to confer with his client.

"Harry, thank the good Lord you are well," said Beck. "But I do not think I can continue in this lifestyle any longer. You will be the death of me—or yourself. And then where would that put either of us, I ask you. Now, what have you done this time? Do you require legal counsel?"

Houdini skewered his manager with his piercing gaze. "Martin, never mind that now. I will look after myself; I need *you* to look into a few things for me while I am, ahem, tied up at the moment." He indicated the wicked-looking handcuffs that adorned his wrists.

Sgt. Bolt, with a spiritedly mischievous gleam in his eye, had introduced Houdini to a pair of handcuffs that defied easy explanation. More like a miniature "iron maiden" torture device of old, the incarceratory device encompassed nearly every inch of the magician's hands as well as his wrists, making for what the policeman called a "Houdini-proof wonder."

"Achh, Harry," moaned Beck. "What have you gotten yourself into, my boy?"

Houdini ignored the question. "However you can, you must uncover more information of the Lyceum's history, going back to, say, the early part of the previous century, and, more specifically, the Mannfreds' ownership of the place. You understand, Martin?"

The sad-faced manager knew full well when it was quite useless to argue or debate with his charge. He nodded and then turned to leave, his marching orders received and clear.

"Oh, hello Miss Mannfred," said Beck, tipping his hat to Houdini's latest guest, arriving stage left.

"Oh, Mr. Houdini—whatsoever will I do with you?"

"My being a gentleman *and* a scholar prevents me from answering that delightful question, my dear," said the young man, amusement reflecting in his eyes. "Perhaps we can address that at a later date. I'm afraid I have my, err, hands full at the present time."

He waggled his handcuffs at the young woman, hoping that he appeared, for once, at a disadvantage and therefore in a sympathetic light to Rose.

She, throwing propriety to the wind, grasped his extended fingers in her own warm hands and placed her forehead on the bars of Houdini's cell. Sighing, Rose tried to explain what had happened at the theatre.

"My uncle threw all of my cousins out of the building. Just like that; almost a hundred years of family relations, gone in an instant…"

Houdini narrowed his eyes at the girl. "Two sides of the same family, ostensibly, yet split by national heritage, British and Italian?"

"Yes. There was a marriage, long ago, that brought us all together, but somewhere in the past came a division. I don't know all the details—we Mannfreds do not speak of it openly—but there is a long-standing enmity that stems from, I gather, a single person."

Houdini considered that. "And this…enmity has led to, what? Sabotage? Arson? Murder, even? Astounding!"

"I feel I know my cousins, as we call them, well, and I cannot imagine any of them wanting to harm us or the theatre, but my father feels as if there is a relation we do not know of that is directing the troubles…

"And my friend, the ghost, is very disturbed by it all."

~ↄ%ᴄ~

There would be no further opportunity for Houdini to plum the depths of Rose's knowledge, for Sgt. Bolt cleared his throat rather noisily behind the girl just then and interrupted their tête-à-tête.

"Visiting hours have come to a close, Miss Mannfred," announced the ungainly officer. "I doubt if your father would care much for your continuing…associations with this criminal. Be on your way, then."

Rose straightened herself and took a few steps backwards. She smiled sweetly at Bolt and nodded demurely, then turned as if to exit the station, catching Houdini's eye briefly but then looking away.

Bolt neared the bars of the little cell and leered mockingly at the magician. The policeman felt as if he had been exceedingly thorough in searching his prisoner's person and removing anything that could possibly aid Houdini in one of his famous escapes.

"You're not in front of a mindless audience now, my fine fellow. You're not in any position for adulation or applause—you're in *my* jail cell wearing *my* special 'cuffs and there you will *stay*. Done and done."

The uniformed man spun on his heel before the magician could snap off a retort. It didn't look particularly spectacular for a wondrous vanishment, he mused to himself. But he would think of something…

Suddenly, the lovely countenance of Rose materialized once more in front of him. Wordlessly, and quite by surprise to Houdini, she reached through the bars and, placing her hand on the back of his head, drew his face to the bars.

Then, she pressed her lips to his and kissed him.

"Rosalina…" breathed Houdini through the kiss. "Italian and British, trapped between two worlds."

The girl released him and then a sad, weary smile spread across her pretty features. Some understanding seemed to pass between the two young people.

In a moment, she was gone, leaving Houdini with the lingering taste of her on his lips and a revived yearning for freedom.

~ↄ%ᴄ~

He soldiered through the snickering scattered around the room and its officers, concentrating on Sgt. Bolt's desk. There, he observed his nemesis conferring with Chief Nelly over a late-night snack; what they were saying was too low for him to discern, unfortunately. Houdini guessed they might be speaking about himself. Let them, he thought. He'd bigger fish to fry.

"Gentlemen," he announced to those assembled. "I now take my leave. Magic is in the air, and I've precious little to spare on you."

Houdini kicked forward with one foot, as if to propel something beyond his cell. Suddenly, a billowing cloud issued forth, almost instantly obscuring the magician and his handsome, smiling face.

The policemen yelped in surprise, sprang up from their chairs and desks. A loud click and then a thump on the wooden floor could be heard from the vicinity of their prisoner's cell, and then the distinctive clank of the barred door being unlocked and flung open.

"Stop him! Stop him!" yelled Bolt. Chief Nelly could also be heard to issue some command or another, but the room was immersed in chaos; nothing of the sort had ever happened at the Bow Street station—nor any other London precinct, to be precise.

When finally the first Bobby made his way haltingly through the noxious, thick cloud, he found the cell quite empty and the amazing Houdini very much gone.

Outside the station, in an alley at the rear of the building, a door opened onto the squalid area and through it stepped the young magician. He dusted off his tailored suit and wiped the dirt from his hands. A slight smile still played around his face.

He would have to remember such an escape for his act—a key passed along through a kiss? Most clever. Not for the first time, Houdini pondered the idea of adding a female accomplice to his growing stage act, but such a decision could wait for a better time.

A bustling cacophony issued forth from the station just then, sending the performer into hiding behind a stacking of wooden crates off to one side in the darkened alley. He peered around the edge of one such crate, attempting to espy his pursuers.

Several men issued forth from the door he'd just come through. Interestingly, not all of them were policemen; a few of them looked to be local toughs. Curious, Houdini strained to pick up on their babbling conversation as they looked all around them for their prey.

What he heard there and then chilled him to his marrow.

Alarmed, Houdini bit his lip and fought back on his natural urge to thrash the men. Far more was now at stake and he could waste no time in animalistic fisticuffs—despite the men's fair earning of such a beating. To his great relief, the mob hurried off down the alleyway. Houdini saw them turn a corner not fifty feet down from his position and then got up to continue with his bid for freedom. He jogged in the opposite direction and to a most wondrous find.

Just two buildings down from the police station, he spied his vehicle for escape. Quite literally, in fact.

There, leaning up against the dirty bricks that defined one section of the alleyway, sat a motorcycle.

Houdini saw instantly that it was one of the German models, most likely a Hildebrand & Wolfmüller. His eyes coveted the conveyance's two-cylinder water-cooled four-stroke engine and he promised himself there and then that if he lived through the present adventure he'd make haste in purchasing one for himself.

But at that stressful moment, Houdini saw fit to borrow the one at hand.

He jumped on the motorcycle, gleaned the operation of its ignition and fired up its engine. Suddenly, a shout came to his ears and he looked down the alleyway to see four of the men who he'd seen exit the station pointing at him and racing in his direction.

Houdini raced the engine of the little motorcycle and throttled it into action. With a stomach-upsetting lurch, the vehicle sprang forward. Within moments, the magician was steering it down the alley and into the street beyond, leaving his pursuers very much in the lurch.

Though fairly unfamiliar with the too-often-labyrinthine streets of London, Houdini got his bearings in rapid time and sped off towards Wellington Street and the Lyceum Theatre. With the wind whipping through his dark hair and the tails of his frock coat unfurled, he resolved to send Martin Beck back later with the motorcycle and a few pounds for its owner's troubles.

He also prayed he was not too late in arriving at the theatre and halting the wicked machinations that were descending upon it.

Still dark in the wee early morning hours, the streets were more or less kind to the magician and he finally pulled up to the Burleigh Street side entrance of the Lyceum. He turned off the motorcycle's engine and, leaning it against a post, left the vehicle behind to find Rose.

The young woman's life was in dire peril. Houdini would not, could not allow that.

He found the door locked, but easily picked the lock in a matter of seconds. Inside, the theatre was pitch black; overall the feeling was of a mausoleum, a home for the dead. The magician shook off the foreboding sensation and hurried through the dark, looking for anyone who could tell him the whereabouts of Miss Mannfred. Hearing voices somewhere ahead of him, he increased his pace, mindful of obstructions in the unfamiliar surroundings. His night vision was keen, he thought, but he couldn't risk anything slowing him down.

Hurrying to the opposite side of the immense theatre, Houdini paused and strained to discern the direction from which the voices issued. A brief, female shout brought him to bear on their location and he ran towards what he felt was to be a situation not much to his liking.

The magician burst through the doors of what he guessed to be the dressing rooms for the theatre's performers. There, he witnessed a very distressing scene, the latest in a production he would not willingly have ever patronized on the stage.

Stoker, his hands gripping Rose's arms, pinning them to her sides, looked over in shock at Houdini's entrance, panic in his eyes and sweat on his brow. The girl's own eyes bored into Houdini's, pleadingly, desperately.

～♋～

Somewhere in the city, a man stood alone in front of a portrait. It showed a woman, stern, imperious, in a high-necked collar and Spartan surroundings.

"It is almost at its end, Mama," said the man, raising a glass of wine to the painting. "The saga. For you, for Sophia, for all who have been ignored and for all who have suffered.

"This I do for you all."

～♋～

Houdini leapt across the room and inserted himself between Stoker and the girl.

He grabbed the Lyceum's manager by his lapels and then pushed the man backwards, away from Rose. It was, he realized, the second time within several hours that he had approached a physical altercation with Stoker.

"Houdini, no!" yelled Rose, grasping the magician's shoulders and upper arms from behind. "Its all right—he-he didn't mean it..."

Houdini looked over at Stoker, who'd fallen against a table and was trying to recover himself, and then to Rose. "My dear, you are in immediate danger—I have no real reason to trust this man or his intentions!"

"Yes, yes!" gulped the portly manager. "Dammit all, yes! She *is* in danger! That's what I was trying to tell her! She needs to leave here, now!"

Houdini shook his head in disbelief. The man had been acting queer since they'd first met and he couldn't exactly divine his connection with Rose Mannfred, which troubled him greatly. Better to be wary of him and get the girl to safety.

"Come along with me, please, Rose," said Houdini. "I don't know the source of Mr. Stoker's information, and frankly I don't care. He may be too deep in your uncle's pocket to be able to see clearly."

At that, Stoker's face grew livid and he clenched and unclenched his fists in spasms of fury. The magician drew the girl behind himself with one arm while keeping the other free to fend off any potential threat from the theatre's manager.

"You," hissed Stoker through clenched teeth, "have absolutely *no* comprehension of what you say!"

The performer saw that something had slipped away in the man, something that once acted as a curtain or a shield for Stoker to hide his true feelings, his inner self, from the world. The wild look of anger and desperation on his face gave Houdini pause.

"Do you know," said Stoker, enunciating each word, each syllable, "what I've been caught in the middle of? This…*struggle* has been going on for *years*, since long before I came to work here. It has been an unholy strain on me, to stay neutral - a strain that I'm sure has taken years off my life!

"I-I want to write! That is all I want to do now! I am a published author, for God's sake—I have had enough of all this…this petty bickering and bull-headed stubbornness! I have had enough of being in the middle of these people and their war!"

"But, it is the Italian side of the family that is behind the majority of the troubles, yes?" asked Houdini.

Stoker nodded, his fury ebbing. "Yes, yes; but Roger Mannfred is also to blame. Oh, Rose, I am sorry to say that…"

The young woman stood resolute in the face of the accusation. Houdini observed that her hands were shaking and marveled at the forces she was marshalling within herself.

"Look at the cost," he heard Stoker say. "Look at the bloody cost…Rose's parents…God bless them…"

"My mother and father," Rose told the magician. "They were killed in a carriage accident five years ago."

"And, by your beautiful name, I would guess that your mother was of Italian heritage?"

"Yes," said the girl quietly, her eyes glistening. "I miss them so much... Bram believes they were murdered, you see."

Abruptly, the wooden door to the room exploded inward in a shower of splinters. Two men stood in the doorway—rough-looking and dark, they wore caps pulled down nearly covering their eyes and oily-looking jackets. The lead man, presumably he who kicked in the door, sneered at Houdini and Stoker.

"*Dacci la ragazza*," growled the man in Italian. *Give us the girl.*

Rose, who understood the language, squeaked at the demand, but did not cringe or fall faint. Regardless, the magician and the manager closed ranks in front of the young woman, effectively forming a barrier between her and the rude interlopers.

"Right," said Stoker to Houdini without turning to look at him. "It's to be a fight then?"

The magician shook his head emphatically. "No, not for you. Take Rose and get her to safety. *Please.*"

Houdini, as properly dressed as a man of the time could be, waded into the two thugs with fists flailing and a look of grim determination on his countenance. He did so with little to no regard for himself, only with the thought of buying Stoker time to spirit away with the girl.

Thankfully, the Lyceum's manager did not quibble and pulled Rose away and through another door.

The first ruffian, who had at least four or five inches on the magician, grunted at Houdini's first blow to his midsection, then savagely head-butted his opponent. His companion, assuming Houdini was well in-hand, slipped away to follow the girl.

The man caught up to Stoker and Rose as they ascended to the theatre's grand balcony. At the top of the stairs he grabbed at the girl, catching the hem of her dress in a meaty paw and, giving the material a violent snap, brought her to her knees. Stoker yelled and rushed up to their assailant, swinging his fists in a wild tangle of blows. None of them landed; with a lightning-fast jab, the thug connected with Stoker's jaw and sent the portly manager spinning backwards and into a large potted fern.

He then turned his murderous attentions to Rose Mannfred.

A moment later Houdini stumbled from the room Stoker and the girl had fled, bloodied and bruised. He let the broken remnants of a chair slip from his fingers; behind him, on the floor, lay his unconscious adversary.

He then heard Rose scream.

Flying through the corridors of the Lyceum, he followed the sound and the palpable smell of fear to a grand staircase and mounted it, three steps at a time. At the top, he could just make out, in the darkness, the prone form of Rose with the second ruffian bending over her, gloved hands clutching like tongs for her throat.

"Rose!" he cried, alarm surging through every inch of his body. "Good Lord, Rose!"

The girl jerked her head to the side to glimpse Houdini's charge, then tightly closed her eyes. She kicked out once, twice, in primal defiance at her assailant.

To the magician's astonishment, he witnessed the amazing sight of Rose, skirts and petticoats askew, lashing out with both her high-top, buttoned shoes and connecting solidly with the thug's solar plexus. Houdini heard something snap.

The man grunted, fell backwards—and toppled over the balcony railing to the floor far below.

Houdini rushed to the young woman and swept her up off the floor and into his arms. She was stiff to the touch at first, but within seconds she began to melt and then to sob.

Through the perfume of Rose's hair, which clouded Houdini's face as held the girl, he looked at Stoker stepping towards him, rubbing his jaw. The manager stared back at the magician with heavily-lidded, serious eyes.

"Come," he said quietly. "She still may be in danger—I know where we can hide her."

~✤~

The room thrilled Houdini. Stepping through its door, sequestered in a long-unused section of the immense building, the magician felt as if he had traveled back in time to witness a bygone era of theatre history.

Beautifully framed posters adorned the walls, covering almost every square inch of them. Houdini saw grand advertisements for many of the great operas and the names of famous singers and performers—all of them Italian. He traced the names with his finger, with the thought that perhaps by doing so he might somehow transfer a small parcel of their success and fame to himself.

"What is this place?"

Here was the rich tapestry of Italian opera, beautiful music and the kind of grand tradition of the stage that Houdini loved.

"What is this place?" he inquired of Stoker. "It seems a…shrine, of sorts."

The Lyceum's manager closed the door quietly and latched it. He listened, one ear to the wood, for a moment. "Yes, I suppose that's one way to describe it. I found it a few years ago—it had been sealed off as if never to be used or seen again."

Rose fell in love with the room the moment she entered it. Houdini could see her entire demeanor change when the posters and opulent— though dusty—furnishings filled her eyes, from horror at the death of her assailant to awe and wonder over the room.

"Look here," announced Houdini. "These posters. They date back to the very early 1800s, but there seems to be none later than…the 1870s?"

Stoker nodded. "1877, in fact. I have studied this room many times since finding it. Further, there was a fire here that year, the year before I entered into my position as manager."

Houdini could also see that one name was repeated on many of the colorful cards up until about 1834, that of the diva Sonia Mannelli. He wondered aloud at that.

"Ah," said Stoker, running his hand over his beard. "One of the most accomplished and famous of the Italian singers of her generation. She suffered a vocal injury at the height of her career and retired. Died about, what? Nine years ago or so? Signora Mannelli was a distant cousin of the…"

"What?" asked the magician.

"…of the Mannfreds. Who, I'm told, ascended to ownership of the Lyceum in 1834, when it was rebuilt after a devastating fire."

"Some things," announced Houdini, gesturing broadly to the stilted air around them, "are becoming clearer now. I feel we are on the precipice of illumination."

Stoker admitted he didn't know too overly much about Sonia Mannelli— the magician inquired as to relatives, but the theatre manager continued to claim ignorance. Houdini scrutinized his erstwhile accomplice in the sordid affair and once again struggled to come to a conclusion about him.

The room, his relationship with Rose, his late-night sojourns, the ghost—Bram Stoker posed too many questions and far too few answers.

"This room is not the demesne of an older person, such as Sonia was when she passed," Rose said suddenly. "Look about us - this is a young person's sanctuary."

"But whose?" Houdini asked her, in admiration of her observation.

"That," noted Stoker, "is the question. I propose we...we conduct a séance to find out."

———✺———

Rose seemed eager to go along with Stoker's idea. As if reading Houdini's mind, while the theatre manager arranged a table and chairs for the séance, she whispered to the magician that Stoker had always been very kind to her and that they'd become friends.

This satisfied some of the performer's ill feelings the man, but he retained his skepticism as to his purpose behind the purported "raising of the dead."

Not thirty seconds after sitting down and linking hands around the table, the room grew chilly. Houdini attributed it to a drafty old building. Stoker seemed to think the cold air signaled the arrival of a spirit.

Came a scratching noise off in a far corner. Then, a tinkling noise, not unlike a tiny bell. Houdini said nothing, biding his time and telling himself he could afford to squander several minutes to keep Rose safe and hid away in the sealed-off room.

"Is there a spirit present?" intoned Stoker. "Please - we are friends. Come and make yourself known to us."

A muffled rapping came to their ears. It seemed to emanate from behind Stoker. Houdini felt Rose squeeze his hand, sensed her shiver. He sighed to himself, frowning in the darkness.

The magician had conducted a few séances in his career, such as it was at the time. He knew his way around flummoxing easily-susceptible people who yearned to contact their deceased loved ones, but he'd halted the practice early on, not wanting to continue in such an unworthy vein.

"Yes," he heard Stoker say quietly. "Yes, someone is here with us. Please, tell us who you are."

The cold continued, but no other sounds were heard after the request.

"If you cannot speak, then knock once for 'yes,' twice for 'no' and three times if you are unsure. Is this your room?"

One knock. Houdini guessed that Stoker had removed his shoe and rapped on the wood floor with his heel.

"Are you a member of the Mannelli family?"

One knock. The magician itched to dive under the table and prove his theory.

"Was Sonia Mannelli a relation of yours?"

Another single knock, clear and distinct. Houdini's mind raced; if the theatre man was hoaxing them, what did he stand to gain by it? Rose's attentions? Her loyalty? Surely he couldn't imagine he'd be able to win over the magician himself?

"If only," sighed Stoker. "We could find out this spirit's own name…"

"Its Sofia," said Rose. "Sofia Mannelli, daughter of Sonia."

Houdini decided that Stoker had somehow previously fed Rose that information and the intense air of the séance had brought it to the surface of the girl's thoughts. Still, he bit his tongue and urged the man to continue.

All at once, he felt a blast of even colder air on his person and looked up to see a face appear out of the darkness, just over Rose's right shoulder.

It was a young woman's face; pretty, but wan, it represented a girl of about Rose's age, with hair set in a style from decades past and a Roman cast to the nose and mouth.

After the initial surprise, Houdini's estimation of Stoker's abilities increased. Obviously, the man had arranged for an actress to wait in the room and "spirit" herself into the circle as the faux-séance escalated. Perhaps Stoker had pulled off this trick many times before.

He hesitated, weighing the benefits of exposing Stoker, but ultimately Houdini again made no move to act. The lovely Rose was engaged and, for the moment, forgetting the events of the attack from before. For her sake, he chose not to upset the table.

Rose sucked in a quivering breath and raggedly let it out again. The magician called her name.

"I'm all right, Houdini," she replied. "I'm fine. Somehow, it's almost as if I can hear Sofia's thoughts. It-it is the same fashion in which we've…talked before…"

Damn and blast the man, Houdini railed inwardly. How was he doing this? His professional curiosity would surely get the best of him and he'd throttle the secret from Stoker.

"Sofia," said Rose, hesitantly. "Can you tell me…how did you die?"

Watching the ghostly apparition closely, Houdini saw it waver in the darkness, as if a stereopticon slide losing its focus.

"A fire," announced the girl, her hand squeezing Houdini's ever more tightly. "Oh, my dear, no…"

The magician remembered Stoker then, and, looking at the man, found him staring intently at Rose. Perhaps, reasoned Houdini, we have a true mesmerist in our midst.

"She-she says…she says her brother is responsible."

The words came down into the middle of the little group like hammer blows. But, before either Stoker or Houdini could pose any other questions, Rose spoke up once again, this time with steely determination.

"Sofia, Sofia!" she called out. "Please—tell me!

"Were my own parents murdered?"

No further words came from Rose's perfect lips. The ghostly face behind her began to fade. Houdini, momentarily dumbfounded, watched as it disappeared completely, back into the shadows. With it went the chilly air and the feeling of gloom that had pervaded the room from the moment they had taken their seats around the table.

The magician fumed. He could not comprehend why Stoker, a respectable theatre manager and alleged author would go to such lengths to fool an innocent girl and cause her such tumult. It strained his faith in humanity, and yet he had allowed it to play out, telling himself it was a relatively harmless bit of flummery.

"Mr. Stoker," said Houdini, standing up. "I question your motives here, and your odd sense of the dramatic. Why did you not feel you could simply tell us of the Mannelli family and their tragedies, instead choosing to upset Rose with this…this hoax?"

The portly man also stood, his face gone red again and cheeks puffing out. "You-you think I faked this up?" He pointed at the table, at Rose. "You're a damn fool, then! I knew nothing of what this Sofia told us! Until now, I knew her only as a spectral figure, one who has resisted all my previous attempts to communicate with her!"

"I call your integrity into question," spat Houdini. "And your standing as a gentleman. To think you'd put on this little show just to—"

"Stop! Stop it, both of you!"

The two men glared at each other and then turned to look upon Rose Mannfred. Her eyes red and wet, she stared them both down in turn, then addressed Houdini.

"My friend," she said, taking the magician's hand in hers. "I'm sorry all of this has angered you. Please don't be confused…I'm sure we can make some sense of it."

Houdini grimaced. "No, I'm not confused, Rosalina. Not anymore. I know just what to do now."

⌒ↄၛౖౖ౮⌒

In the middle his act, Houdini smiled to himself. It was going well, very well, and he moved the performance along and into its final show-stopping moments.

The Lyceum stage seemed to suit him well and he wished he'd been able to book it for an honest, full show. As it was, he played that evening to a smaller, captive audience, one carefully chosen.

Houdini looked out into that audience as he explained about a bit of rope and its supposed mystical qualities. There he saw many engaged faces, enjoying his magical act and eager for even more magic and illusion.

After the séance in the forgotten room, Houdini proposed he'd perform his entire magical revue for a select audience in the famous theatre, a kind of thank-you to the owners for allowing him to tour the premises and to commemorate their own upcoming—and perhaps final—extravaganza. The magician wished to invite the Lyceum family, the entire cast and crew of *The Merchant of Venice,* a few local notables and the officers of the Bow Street police garrison. It would be a nice, well-rounded selection, he mused.

Martin Beck, after conferring with Houdini, made entries to Sir Roger Mannfred about such a performance, but the Lyceum's owner bulled and crowed and issued an abject refusal. It took many hours of talk from Stoker and Rose to convince him otherwise. The show would go on, but with the tacit disapproval of the cantankerous man.

Rose, bless her heart, had offered to stand in as stage assistant for the performance, but Houdini wouldn't allow himself the temptation of her presence on stage. Besides, he reasoned that she'd be safer in the audience, if his scheme went off as planned.

"Ladies and gentlemen," he announced, resplendent in glorious evening dress at center stage. "I thank you most warmly and sincerely for your kind indulgence tonight. I think, perhaps, you have seen that magic is all about us, waiting for the opportunity to amaze and, yes, even inform us."

There, gazing up at the young man from the front row, were Martin Beck, Bram Stoker, Rose and Roger Mannfred, the Mannfred sons, the Lyceum orchestra conductor, *The Merchant of Venice*'s lead performers, Sgt. Bolt of the London police force and his superior, Chief Nelly.

"Now, for my final mystification of the evening—I give you An International Spectacle!"

Houdini raised both arms, his palms open and wide, and as he spread his hands out from his body, there was a pop and a flash that followed them through the air above his head. There, somehow, hanging in mid-air, was a string of colorful pennants representing the flags of several nations. Their colors seemed to glow, vibrant and rich, and they fluttered daintily in an impossible breeze. Among the countries represented were the United States, England, Germany, Spain, France, Russia and many others—but not Italy.

Houdini scrutinized the faces of his audience, gauging their reactions.

One face, one set of eyes in particular, told the magician exactly what he wanted to know, confirming his suspicions.

"I will need an assistant or two from the audience—no, not you, my dear Rose…" A good-natured chuckle of mirth spread through the crowd. Rose blushed prettily and brought her hand down.

"Ah, Sir Roger," noted Houdini. "Just the ticket! If you please, sir. Come up and give me a hand with this, will you? And, let's see…ah, Chief Nelly? If you would be so kind to accompany Sir Roger? That's a good fellow—our illustrious owner may need more help than he knows…"

Mannfred frowned and shook his head, but his niece prodded him on and he reluctantly mounted the steps to the stage. Chief Nelly followed, smiling and in good humor. He patted Sir Roger on the back and whispered an encouragement.

"There we are," said Houdini to the two men, arranging them just to one side of a table that was adorned with a few lit candles, a set of handcuffs, a top hat and the flags hanging over the entire assemblage. "Everything in its place and a place for everything."

The magician turned to his audience. "I have something to admit to, ladies and gentlemen. There is no 'International Spectacle.' There is only this: the exposing of a criminal."

A gasp from the crowd came to Houdini's ears. Then murmurings of curiosity.

"*Non è così*, Signor Mannelli? You didn't care for the omission of the Italian flag—I could see it on your face. I also observed your fine Italian boots at the station, and your half-eaten meal of *ravioli*. That tipped me off, too."

Chief Nelly took a step forward. "My full admiration to you, Signor Houdini. But, you were wrong—it is indeed a spectacle you offer us after all."

Before the magician could properly react, the chief pushed Sir Roger backwards roughly with one hand and then pointed to the audience with his other. "Look there," he commanded.

Cold blue steel glinted in the theatre's lights. A revolver, pointed at Rose Mannfred's right temple by a man who crouched behind her. The girl's eyes widened, but she remained silent.

Houdini, dampening down his fury at the quite un-gentlemanly act, shook his head in disgust. "All this, Mannelli—all this for the cause of petty nationalism?"

The chief grimaced. "You-you think this is simply because of *nationalism*? Houdini, you disappoint me now.

"This is *revenge*! Revenge for my family and for my dear mother! We Mannellis have conducted sorties of vengeance for *decades* now against these Mannfreds—and tonight is the final bow for them and their precious theatre...and yes, we strike a blow for Italy, too."

"Fires throughout the years," said Houdini, fixing the man with a deadly serious gaze. "Other acts of harassing destruction. Including death. Rose's parents for—"

"They *dared* to marry!" screeched Mannelli. "After many years of separation, they thought to reconcile the two halves by wedding and producing a *child*!"

The magician looked at Rose. She stared back at him, nodding slightly. He gave her a little smile and what he hoped was a look of compassion and understanding.

"And Sonia Mannelli's daughter," noted Houdini, turning back to the chief. "Was she somehow in the way? Your own sister?"

Mannelli's entire countenance sank. He produced a revolver from a pocket and cocked it. "Damn you," he hissed. "Damn you...that was a mistake..."

Houdini lunged at him, suddenly. Then, the entire theatre erupted into unbridled chaos.

The chief caught the leaping magician with a glancing blow to the side of his face. Houdini grunted but his forward momentum was enough to send him careening into his target. The two men went down in a tangle of limbs. Mannelli's gun went off loudly and Sir Roger yelped and was flung backwards like a ragdoll.

The entire audience leapt out of their seats all at once. Screams and cries of outrage and panic filled the theatre as people tried to flee towards exits and found themselves enmeshed with those others around them.

Sgt. Bolt flung himself at the man who held Rose Mannfred at gunpoint. The young woman aided her would-be rescuer by chopping at the man's hand with her own—her actions caught the thug by surprise and he was wrestled to the floor by the ungainly sergeant.

A savage kick to Houdini's stomach allowed Mannelli the upper hand. He rose to his feet and turned to look for his gun. Spotting the candles on the table, he upended the entire scenario into a nearby stage curtain. The material caught fire instantaneously and was engulfed in moments.

The chief swiveled around to catch a blow from Houdini on the jaw. The man staggered and fell against the burning curtains. The young magician sprung back as he watched, mesmerized, as the former police officer's uniform ignited and was soon fully ablaze.

Mannelli screamed like all the devils in Hell.

Houdini whipped off his evening coat and threw it over the burning man and then knocked him to the stage floor to attempt to squelch the flames. He heard another scream, a female's, and looked up to see an immense swatch of fiery curtains raining down upon him.

Years of performing incredible escapes had honed fine-tuned senses and hair-trigger agility in the magician. He rolled out of the path of the conflagration at the very last moment and found himself falling off the edge of the stage and into the orchestra pit below.

Then, all went dark.

~◊◊◊~

A beautiful angle swam into his view. No, he thought, if swimming, it must be a mermaid. Or a Nereid. Yes, that would be nice.

"Houdini," came a course voice, knocking the magician from his reverie. "Harry, my boy—are you alive? We have other commitments!"

"Yes, Martin," said Houdini weakly. "I will endeavor to stand up and prepare for the next show. Simply allow me a year or two to do so...."

Rose Mannfred, in the role of a Nereid, hugged him then. "Oh, Houdini. It's terrible...horrible..."

She sat back so that the young man could rise up on his elbows to see what could be seen. The sight that greeted him was indeed a horrific one, a scene plucked from Dante's *Inferno*.

The Lyceum Theatre was ablaze. Great tongues of fire poured from its doors and windows. From Houdini's vantage point across the street, he knew immediately that there would be no saving the venerable old palace. There would be no final performance on its famous stage.

Gathered around him was Martin Beck, haggard and worried; Rose, pain etched upon her lovely young face; Bram Stoker, morose; and, surprisingly, a walking Sir Roger Mannfred. The man clutched at his side with one hand and kept smoothing back his hair with the other. He watched as fire ate away at his theatre, bit by bit.

Stoker turned to Houdini. "You were right—Chief Nelly had changed his name from Mannelli years ago, to hide his heritage. Seems he set the fire that accidentally killed his sister Sofia..."

"Yes," nodded Houdini. "Martin looked into it and found out that Sonia Mannelli had a son as well as a daughter. And that she was near-maniacal in her devotion to all things Italian. She must have been beyond fury when the Lyceum dispensed with nothing but English opera back in 1834."

"My-my parents?" asked Rose, looking intently at the magician. "He killed them?"

"Oh, Rose, I am so sorry. Yes, yes, that is what it seems to be—they were the Romeo and Juliet of this drama. Mannelli was poisoned by his mother's vitriol over her own lost career and the leeching away of her Italian heritage from her beloved stomping grounds, the Lyceum. He obviously carried on her work after she died, directing his ne'er-do-wells under cover of an assumed name…and the upstanding life of a policeman."

Roger Mannfred suddenly turned to face the others, a bewildered look on his face. "We were friends," he said quietly. "The bastard had me fooled—for years. Striking at us in secrecy, bringing us to-to *this*."

Houdini struggled to his feet, a dark cloud floating down over his own features and anger stoked within his heart. He took Mannfred by his lapels and shook him.

"You are as much at fault for this day as he was!"

"Houdini!" gulped Stoker. "Whatever do you mean? Sir Roger— responsible for the loss of his own theatre, his own brother and sister-in-law?"

"Nationalism may be found on either side of the tally, my dear Stoker. I am prideful of my origins, like many others, but to walk its path in unswerving temerity is beyond foolish—in my opinion." He glared at Sir Roger. "It leads to blindness. It leads to petty wars, like this one."

Mannfred could only stand there, mouth gaping, eyes wide with realization and a dollop of fright.

"We-we shall rebuild," he whispered, finally. "The Lyceum will reopen! I swear it!"

Houdini released the man's coat, and smoothed it down as he stepped back. "Swear rather an allegiance to those who need you *now*, right this tragic moment, such as your employees.

"And honor your family. Your *entire* family."

⌒϶ϘϾ⌒

Five days later, Houdini and his manager stood in the lobby of their London hotel, supervising the loading of the magician's numerous bags and boxes and trunks. They were both somber and reflective.

Rose Mannfred had not come to see him since the destruction of the Lyceum, nor had he gone to pay a visit on her.

He was quite sure he wouldn't know what to say to the young woman. She had lost much, and learned even more—what could one say that would matter more than that? Ultimately, Houdini had decided to give her some room to settle her thoughts and not be saddled with an itinerant prestidigitator to muck things up further.

"Well, Harry," said Beck. "I am sure you will feel better at the next stop, on the next stage. You always do. I could set my watch by it."

Houdini picked up a valise and went to climb aboard the waiting cab. He placed his foot upon the step of the hansom and was about to pull himself up when a sweet voice whispered in his ear.

"Do you believe in ghosts now?"

He smiled and turned to find himself in the bone-crunching embrace of Miss Rose Mannfred. She smelled and felt wonderful.

"Well, if you don't relax your grip on me, I'm sure I will discover the truth first hand…"

"Oh, Houdini. I've missed you. Why didn't you come and see me?"

The magician looked deep into her dark eyes, seeing a measure of pain and suffering that still lingered. He smiled at the beautiful red rose she had tucked into her hair.

"Repeat performances tend to depress me. I make my bows and then move along, Rosalina."

She narrowed her eyes at him, wondering at the deeper meaning behind his words, but said nothing.

"What will you do now with your life?" Houdini asked her, taking the rose from her hair and fixing it on his jacket.

She put on an air of regal bearing and smiled haughtily. "I thought perhaps I'd become an actress. Don't you think that would suit me?"

"I'm not so sure it would, but I suppose, with you, all things are possible, my dear."

She nodded. "All the world's a stage, oh Great Houdini. All the world's a stage…"

Rose kissed him, a lingering pressing of her soft lips to his cheek, leaving behind a wisp of her scent and the memory of the stirring adventure they shared.

"Goodbye, Rosalina. Be well," he told her sincerely, then got into the cab alongside his manager. The girl gazed up at him.

"Thank you for the magic, Houdini."

THE END

ABOUT HOUDINI

Ithink my long-time interest in Harry Houdini began in earnest with the 1976 Paul Michael Glaser TV film THE GREAT HOUDINIS. The film fascinated me on many levels, though I know now that it, of course, only presented an idealized, short-hand version of the famous magician's life and death—but that's okay, because Houdini himself built his larger-than-life persona into an unstoppable, infamous force that continues to this day. And it's that over-the-top persona that brings us to this anthology.

I consider Harry Houdini one of my heroes. He was, I've learned in more recent years, a guy who pulled himself up from humble beginnings with a quick wit and a knack for making a buck, but he was also someone who wouldn't hesitate to have a rival beat up in an alley if he thought they were poaching on his intellectual territory. And yet, I unashamedly count him as one of my heroes. You see, despite his rough edges, Harry possessed a singular drive to be one of the most unique men on the planet, someone who had a deep desire to entertain and to thrill and to mystify—sometimes at the cost of all else.

And he wasn't just a magician. Houdini was the very first person to fly an airplane on the Australian continent, and he was also an author and a film star and serious debunker of spiritualism. He might also have been a spy, if you believe that. Not hard to believe, actually, considering the life Houdini led. If he wasn't escaping jail cells or jumping off of bridges, he was filming movies or traipsing around the globe or speaking out on topics he believed in. Is it any wonder that Ron Fortier of Airship 27 chose this man, of all real-life personalities throughout history, around which to craft a series of pulp adventures?

When Ron proposed the idea, I jumped at it immediately, sure, but then wondered how I'd ever do the real Houdini justice—he was practically a super hero while he lived and he's become an almost supernatural legend since he died. Fortunately, Ron asked his authors to concentrate on the adventurous, mysterious persona that Harry built up over the many years of his incredible career—a career that reads like a pulp novel at points. The hard part would be choosing which of the magician's stunts would make for the coolest action scenes in our stories.

I chose to concentrate on the more ghostly aspects of Houdini's adventures, a subject near and dear to my heart. I spirited up a story that would center around a haunting in an old theater and Ron liked the idea, but suggested I set the tale in the real-life Lyceum Theatre in London and introduce Houdini to a fictionalized version of the famous author of "Dracula," Bram Stoker.

How could anyone say no to that?

So, I started doing my research on the Lyceum and uncovered a treasure trove of information on its long history, items that supplemented my basic story and fleshed out its back-story. The Lyceum you read about in my tale isn't exactly the famous theatre that still exists today in London, but a shadowy silhouette of it that might exist in the alternate universe of a fictional Houdini. So, too, with my Bram Stoker; the man you met in "Houdini Brings the Curtain Down" shares many features with his real-life counterpart, but is a bit more fiction than reality. I really enjoyed writing this Stoker…though I almost wish he and my Houdini had gotten on a bit better. I guess the stress of the situation in which they found themselves didn't exactly lend itself to them becoming bosom buddies, alas.

By the way, the real Stoker was reportedly much like the real Harry Houdini in his outlook towards the supernatural; he wanted to believe, but the evidence to support such a belief was not substantial enough to form a more concrete opinion on the matter.

Research can be one of the most fun aspects of pulp avenues, providing the writer with avenues of exploration that might lead reveal…anything. In my second "chapter," I arranged for Houdini to be waylaid by a ruffian, but I knew that I wanted the fight to have an extra "something" to it. I began to wonder if there was such a thing as European martial arts and in poking around I discovered Italian stick-fighting. Imagine that; never in a million years would I ever have imagined I'd be doing research on the fine art of Italian stick-fighting! Biff! Bam! Pow! And a Zowie for good measure!

You may have noticed that this book's fictional Houdini is not married, though the real-life magician most definitely was, and to a woman he remained with—if not entirely faithful to—until his dying day. By freeing our Houdini from the bonds of matrimony this allows me to create a character like Rosalina Mannfred, and such a character is one of the joys of being a writer.

I wanted to make Rose a fairly balanced co-star, in the sense of making her a young woman of her time yet also a mostly-independent girl who doesn't always shrink from danger and adventure. This wasn't as easy a task as one might think, for I had to think carefully about how she'd react in any given situation and provide the reader with a foundation of belief for all of her actions. I hope, in the end, that Rose appears as both a sympathetic character and a true pulp heroine. I also hope you've grown to like her as much as I have.

I'd like to acknowledge a few books which aided me immensely in my writing of "Houdini Brings the Curtain Down." First and foremost is THE SECRET LIFE OF HOUDINI: THE MAKING OF AMERICA'S FIRST SUPERHERO, by William Kalush and Larry Sloman, a book I first read several years ago and has become my most favorite non-fiction tome of all. I can't recommend it enough. I also accessed useful information in BRAM STOKER: A BIOGRAPHY OF THE AUTHOR OF *DRACULA* by Barbara Belford, a book that provided me with a good glimpse of the writer and the real-life manager of the Lyceum. Thirdly, the images in VICTORIAN AND EDWARDIAN LONDON FROM OLD PHOTOGRAPHS helped me envision the streets and sounds and smells of the city for scenes in my story. I actually propped the book open to a few photographs to look at while I wrote.

Also, while writing my story, I looked into reports that the magician had actually performed in my hometown—sure enough, on three separate occasions, in 1892, 1893 and 1907, Houdini brought his act to our fair city. Sadly, he was scheduled to perform here a fourth time, but died unexpectedly in a Detroit hospital bed shortly before the date of the planned show. There was also one other fascinating fact I uncovered that tickled my fancy: Houdini was once the agent for an acrobat named, of all things, Jim Bard.

For all you completists out there in pulpdom, here are the "chapter" titles for the story—if it had chapter titles, of course: "The Great Mystifier," "The Master Mystery," "The Grim Game," "King of Handcuffs," "Ghost House" and "Metamorphosis."

Big thanks and a tip of the top hat to Captain Ron Fortier for letting me play in Houdini's world, to Susan Littleton for a bit o' help with my Italian, and, as always, to The Little Woman for the best sounding board any writer could ever hope for. This one's for you, too, m'dear.

Jim

JAMES BEARD -Though born a redhead, Jim has struggled with the accompanying adversity and prejudice to achieve his dream of working as a pulp writer. He made his first professional sale in 2002, to DC Comics, and has never looked back; writing is in his blood. He credits his father for introducing him to the heroes and villains who populated the pulps and the comic books of the early Twentieth Century, and he's strived to honor their rich history while always looking for new ways to move them forward

Jim's pulp fiction includes SGT. JANUS, SPIRIT-BREAKER, PRESIDENTIAL PULP, MONSTER ACES, MONSTER EARTH, ZEPPELIN TALES, and CAPTAIN ACTION: RIDDLE OF THE GLOWING MEN. In addition, he also has comic work for DC, Dark Horse, and IDW, and well as creating and editing a book of essays on the 1966 Batman TV series, GOTHAM CITY 14 MILES.

Having survived writing the second Captain Action novel, Jim looks forward to once again flying into action with the good captain to finish the trilogy.

HOUDINI AND THE SPEAR OF DESTINY

BY JAMES PALMER

"If coming events are said to cast their shadows before, past events cannot fail to leave their impress behind them." Madam Helena Petrova Blavatsky

Martin Beck held up three fingers to the man hanging upside down in a tank of water.

The man inside the tank nodded and redoubled his efforts. Three minutes. He had already been submerged for three minutes. Reaching inside the secret compartment in the floor of the tank, hidden from the audience by the riveted metal frame that held the thick glass of the tank in place, he produced a key. Holding it carefully between his outstretched thumb and index finger, he carefully inserted it into the lock on the heavy manacles that bound his wrists. Even after performing this maneuver hundreds of times, there was still the possibility that he could drop the key and lose precious time, and even more precious oxygen.

There was a barely audible click, and the manacle that fettered his right wrist was free. Now able to move more freely, he made short work of the left manacle; it fell to the bottom of the tank with a heavy thunk.

Now Harry Houdini bent his body upward to free his legs, a strenuous maneuver made even more difficult by the pull of gravity and the density of the water. He wouldn't have much longer now; already black spots were starting to dance in front of his vision.

Freeing his ankles would be another matter, for they were each secured by two different and separate padlocks, each chosen by a member of Scotland Yard. He inserted his trusty skeleton key into the first padlock and twisted it. It wouldn't budge.

From the corner of his eye, Houdini saw his agent, Martin Beck, standing at the side of the tank, a hint of worry beginning to line his features.

The magician twisted the key again and the padlock hasp sprung free. He used it on the other padlock before removing both, righting himself, and then shoving the top of the tank open to thrust himself into the life-giving air of the theater.

The small crowd clapped and cheered as a soaking wet Harry Houdini climbed over the side of the tank and dropped to the stage floor, his arms outstretched in triumph, a huge grin upon his face.

His agent gave him a towel, which he wrapped around his short frame with a flourish. Now wearing the towel like a magician's cape, he waved to the small crowd of reporters, photographers, and city dignitaries that had come to see the escapist's special preview showing.

"For a second there I was afraid you wouldn't make it," said Beck in Houdini's ear.

The handcuff king rubbed his wrists. "Don't worry about me, old friend. You know I'd never disappoint a crowd."

"Let me guess. You were cutting it close to heighten the excitement."

Houdini beamed. "Exactly. Now let's do it again. I want to get it under three minutes."

Beck groaned. "You've done it five times since we arrived in Westminster. We can't have you tiring out before your first show tomorrow night."

"I'm not tired. Now let's do it again."

Beck gave a disapproving groan. "Let's get you out of those wet clothes," said Beck. "You're not getting sick on my watch."

The agent put a hand on Houdini's shoulder and led him toward the rear of the stage and his waiting dressing room while the small but vocal crowd continued to cheer.

***

Beck sat in Houdini's chair working a crossword puzzle while the magician changed into an expensive evening suit. As he finished tying his tie, there was a knock at the dressing room door.

Beck looked up at his charge. "I wonder who that could be."

"Well, go and answer it and satisfy our mutual curiosity."

Beck stood, placed his crossword puzzle and pencil in the chair, and went to the door and opened it. An older man wearing a brown tweed suit and wire-rimmed spectacles stood in the doorway, rocking on his heels and running a finger through his thick, bushy mustache, which made him resemble a walrus instead of the most famous author in England.

Houdini smiled. "Doyle! Come in. What did you think of the performance?"

Sir Arthur Conan Doyle stepped into the room. "Splendid as always," said the author.

"That's very kind," said Houdini. "Beck, make sure Doyle gets two tickets to the show tonight."

Beck nodded and offered Doyle something to drink. The author asked for a brandy and sat on a green couch at the other end of the small but well appointed dressing room.

"I didn't come for free tickets, though I accept the gracious offer." Doyle sipped the proffered brandy. "This special preview show was also a very nice surprise."

Once Houdini had finished putting himself back together, he turned and looked at his friend, who was smiling and looking about rather nervously. The author checked the time on his pocket watch attached to his vest by a gold chain and sipped his brandy.

"How was your journey?" Doyle asked.

"Oh, fine, fine. Uneventful. I did some sleight of hand for the other passengers aboard ship on the way here. Though we had quite an adventure at the Lyceum, didn't we, Beck?"

Beck rolled his eyes. "That's putting it mildly."

Doyle nodded sadly. "Yes, I read about the fire. I'm glad no one was injured."

"Tell him about the ghost," said Beck.

"By Jove!" Doyle exclaimed. "You saw a ghost?"

Houdini moved Beck's crossword puzzle and sat down. "Well, it's…"

Just then there was another knock at the door.

"What's this?" said Beck. "Visiting hours?"

Doyle smiled and set his empty glass on a little marble-topped side table and stood. "Oh, that must be the reason I dropped by. I'll let her do the explaining. Mr. Beck, the door, if you please?"

Houdini went to stand beside Doyle while Beck answered the door. They made a strange pair, the taller, older author and the shorter, slightly bow-legged magician.

A young woman with wavy blond hair stood on the other side of the portal, wringing her hands. She scanned the room and locked eyes on Doyle. "Sir Arthur!" she exclaimed. "The attendant out front said I would find you here."

"Come in, please," said Houdini.

"Thank you for coming, Ms. Pierce," said Doyle. "This is Harry Houdini and his agent, Martin Beck."

On being introduced to Houdini she smiled, her green eyes sparkling. Houdini offered his hand and she shook it. "Pleased to meet you. I am Marjorie Pierce."

"I am pleased to make your acquaintance, Ms. Pierce," said Houdini, taking up her hand again and kissing it. "What brings you by this afternoon?"

Marjorie looked to Doyle.

"I haven't told him anything yet, my dear," said the author. "I wanted him to hear the tale in your own words."

"All right," said Marjorie.

"Let's all have a seat," said Houdini. "Beck, move those insufferable crossword puzzles of yours."

Beck picked up the numerous crossword puzzles he had scattered about on the other end of the couch and tossed them aside. Ms. Pierce sat down, with Doyle and Houdini on either side. Beck took the chair recently vacated by Houdini, an exasperated look on his face. His friend and client never could ignore a damsel in distress, and he feared this conversation was going to take them into the jaws of danger once again.

"Well, I think my brother is in trouble. He has fallen in with a spiritualist and has given her a great deal of money. But that isn't what bothers me. Since he started attending this young woman's séances he hasn't quite been the same. I fear for his sanity. I've been to the police, but they said there is nothing they can do."

"I see," said Houdini. "How has your brother's behavior changed?"

"Well, he has started walking in his sleep. He'll get up late at night and march up and down the halls. He bangs things around. He goes into the library and upsets entire shelves of books, knocking them to the floor. He even went into the kitchen and completely rearranged our housekeeper Mrs. Dingle's pots and pans."

"Oh my," said Doyle.

"On one occasion I tried to wake him, but he just looked at me with this blank stare and said he was looking for something, and he couldn't rest until he found it. In the mornings after these events, he's tired and cross and telling everyone they're crazy for accusing him of such nonsense!"

"And this all started about the time he began to see the spiritualist?" asked Houdini.

Marjorie Pierce nodded. "And it's grown much worse."

Houdini looked at Doyle. "What do you make of all this?"

"I've never heard its like in all my days," said the author. "Ms. Pierce knew of my stature in spiritualist circles, and came to me for advice. I told her that there are hundreds of legitimate mediums practicing the noble art of communicating with the dead, but if there is a medium operating under false pretences, then she must be unmasked before she besmirches the entire religion."

Unseen by Doyle, Martin Beck rolled his eyes. Houdini caught the gesture, but made no comment.

"I also told her that there is no one better at ferreting out charlatans than Harry Houdini, and since I knew you were coming to London, I thought I would invite her to ask you for your assistance."

Houdini nodded thoughtfully. "Ms. Pierce, I would love to help you. Tell me who this medium is, and where we can find her."

Beck shot from his chair. "Can I have a brief word? In private?"

Houdini grinned and stood, and the two men went outside the dressing room and closed the door. "I thought I said no more adventures!" said Beck.

"No adventure, just a chance to unmask another phony medium. You knew I was going to see as many as I could while we're here. That's why I invited Doyle to my special performance. I knew he'd try to 'show me the light' as it were by bringing me around to his latest find. But this is something different."

"We don't have time for anymore nonsense. The tour…"

"Will go on as scheduled. Stop worrying so much." Houdini reentered the dressing room and addressed Doyle and their guest.

"I will help you and your brother."

They began to make plans immediately. Marjorie told them everything she knew about the medium, a young woman named Rosemary Watson. She lived with a strange man she referred to as her brother, who called himself Frater Perdurabo. Marjorie heard from her brother that there was another séance planned for tonight. Houdini would go in disguise, so his famous presence would not disrupt the event. Doyle, who was well known in spiritualist circles, would not look out of place, and so didn't need a disguise. Beck insisted on tagging along in order to "watch his investment" and keep Houdini safe. He wanted the magician's first show in London the following evening to be a success.

Marjorie didn't know if her brother would be in attendance or not, but Houdini and Doyle decided that she should not go with them. She excused herself and left the theater.

"What an amazing young woman," Houdini remarked after she had left. "I hope we can help with her brother's predicament."

"I doubt there is any real danger to her brother," said Doyle, patting his friend on the back. "People are often looked upon with suspicion when trying to elevate their minds to a higher plane. Mr. Pierce is simply opening his mind to further possibilities."

"We'll see," said Houdini.

Doyle arched an eyebrow. "Are you telling me, that after all you've witnessed, you still don't believe?"

"I could ask you the opposite," Houdini replied. "I have shown you how these mediumistic effects can be produced through perfectly normal means and unmasked trickster after trickster, and yet you still believe."

"I know what I have seen," said Doyle.

"As do I," Houdini countered.

"Can we stick to the subject at hand, gentlemen?" said Beck, stepping between the two as if they were about to come to blows. "The Pierce case. Let's get this over with so we can get back to the tour!"

Outside the Alhambra Theater, the three men hailed a waiting hansom cab and gave the driver the address Marjorie Pierce provided. Soon they were threading their way through afternoon traffic on the Strand. Houdini stared out the window. He loved London and its grand old architecture, much of it centuries older than anything to be found in the States. They passed Trafalgar Square on their right, with Nelson's Column dominating the scene, the four lions at its base guarding the structure like sentries.

The hansom turned onto Fleet Street. Doyle turned to Houdini, who was already in his disguise of a frock coat and thick-rimmed glasses. "You look ridiculous," the author said, smiling.

Houdini returned the smile. "All part of the show, my friend. All part of the show."

As they clopped down Fleet Street, Houdini thought of all the various newspapers and other news outlets that made up the London press which resided there. The showman in him wondered if he should have a reporter or two tag along to cover this adventure for the papers. Then he thought better of it. He was already in disguise so as to not cause a commotion, and bringing a reporter and photographer along would negate any secrecy he was trying to maintain. He wondered too about Doyle's motives for springing this surprise adventure upon him. The author remained an adamant supporter of spiritualism, a field full of charlatans and the deluded. He also seemed convinced that Houdini himself had some kind of supernatural ability, a notion that the magician had never been able to shake him of.

The carriage reached its destination. Beck paid the fare, and the three men got out. They stood before a large house. Houdini bounded up the wooden steps to the door, followed closely by Doyle and Beck. Houdini was about to ring for the owner of the house when he noticed small placard in the window.

DUE TO DEMAND, THE SCHEDULED SÉANCE HAS BEEN
MOVED TO
EGYPTIAN HALL
170 PICCADILLY, WESTMINSTER
8:00 TONIGHT

"I guess our Miss Watson has made quite a name for herself," said Doyle, smiling broadly.

"So it would seem," remarked Houdini, checking his pocket watch. "We'd better hurry if we want to get a good seat."

The three men knew the Egyptian Hall well, for it had become a major gathering place for both magicians and spiritualists in recent years. They hurried to the end of the walk so they could hail another cab. When one finally stopped for them, it was of the horse and buggy variety.

"Fancy a lift, guv'nors?" said the coachmen sitting high on his box. He was an older, haggard-looking man, resplendent in top hat and tails, leaving Houdini to surmise that he must be working for the tourist trade, taking out-of-towners on a leisurely stroll through the more popular regions neighboring the Strand. At this point, Houdini would take whatever they could get, for the traffic at this hour was horrible.

"Yes, please," said Beck, taking charge. "Can you take us to 170 Piccadilly?"

"The 'gyptian Hall? O course. Hop in."

The three men climbed aboard and the man whistled to his lone dray. The grey beast started off, its hooves clopping loudly on the street while motorcars swerved to move past.

"You gents bound for the spiritual doin's tonight?" asked the coachman.

"Yes," said Doyle amiably. "Do you believe in spiritualism Mr.—?"

"Blair, Sir. Mortimer Blair. And no Sir, can't say that I do, though there are them that no more 'bout such matters than I. No, I jus' like to keep track a what's going on about town."

"Oh, it's very fascinating," said Doyle, warming to the subject. Houdini flashed Beck a look that said they were in for a longer ride than expected.

"Are you one a them mediums, Sir?" asked Blair.

Doyle chuckled. "Oh no, but I have witnessed many mediumistic phenomena. I suppose I am considered an expert on the subject. I am Sir Arthur Conan Doyle."

The coachman almost fell off his box on top of Doyle, who was sitting in the middle. After he righted himself, he turned to squint and gawk at the author. "Gracious me! The most celebrated writer in England sittin' in me 'umble carriage. Wait till the missus hears about this!"

"And this," said Doyle, pointing to his right, "Is the magician and escape artist Harry Houdini."

Mr. Blair made a show of almost falling off his box again and losing his reins in the process. He craned his neck to the right to squint at Houdini. "My hat! Two famous people in a single fare! My missus ain't gonna bloody well believe this, I can tell you. She'll have me up at Bedlam afore the night's out." He gave a deep throaty laugh that threatened to turn into a terrible, racking cough before finally subsiding.

Mr. Blair guided his horse and carriage onto Piccadilly, and soon they arrived at Egyptian Hall, where a crowd of people had assembled outside.

"This is quite a crowd for a simple séance," said Beck as they climbed down.

"I think this is something a bit more elaborate," remarked Houdini as he and Doyle walked toward the building.

When Beck tried to pay their fare, the coachman stopped him. "If the missus found out I took money for ridin' Sir Arthur Conan Doyle and the famous Harry Houdini a couple a steps, she'd nag me nigh until Doomsday. Keep yer money, and if you chaps need a lift while you're in town, just whistle for old Morty, and me an' Nelly here will be there on the double."

Beck nodded as Mortimer Blair, his dray horse Nelly, and their fancy coach clopped out into traffic and loped leisurely up the street toward Piccadilly Circus. "Strange old chap," he said as he caught up with Houdini and Doyle.

"People like him are the salt of the earth," said Doyle. "Now what's with this abominable line?"

The line was shorter than expected. A few people recognized Doyle and graciously allowed the three to move ahead. Once inside the doors the line moved very quickly, threading into one of Egyptian Hall's larger meeting

*"I suppose I am considered an expert on the subject.
I am Sir Arthur Conan Doyle."*

rooms. Houdini, Beck and Doyle found a seat in the last row of chairs near the back. It wasn't Houdini's favorite vantage point for unmasking frauds, but he was determined to make it work. Already his keen eyes scanned the room for anything that might assist a medium in her trickery. At the front of the room was a makeshift platform or stage, upon which a table draped in blood red cloth sat. When everyone was seated, the electric lights dimmed, eliciting a low murmur from the audience. Then a young girl appeared from somewhere in the wings, walking out and ascending the platform and taking a seat at the table, facing the audience.

The crowd of men and women cheered.

"They've seen this show before," Houdini said to Doyle and Beck.

The girl said nothing, simply sat there, her hands resting upon the table.

A few minutes later a young man in his twenties appeared. He was thin, with a shock of unruly dark hair, and wearing a dark, expensive-looking suit. "Good evening, acolytes," he said in a deep voice, his British accent thick.

"Acolytes?" breathed Houdini. Doyle looked at the magician and shrugged.

"Tonight you will once again bear witness to the parting of the veil between this world and the next. Sister Watson, are you ready?"

"Yes, Brother Perdurabo," said the girl, her eyes remaining fixed on the audience.

"Have you heard of this man before?" whispered Houdini.

Doyle looked at his friend. "No. Never. Though he looks familiar."

The man climbed the platform and stood in front of the table, his arms outstretched, head down, and eyes closed. "Spirits, we are grateful to you for this new revelation, this breaking down of the walls between two worlds. We thirst for another undeniable message from beyond, another call of hope and guidance to the human race at this, the time of its greatest affliction. Can we receive another sign from our friends from beyond?"

At this a cold wind blew through the room, causing the audience to collectively shiver. Seemingly satisfied, the man, this Brother Perdurabo, stepped down from the platform.

Ms. Watson closed her eyes. Her body began to sway back and forth, and there was a rumble low in her throat.

When her eyes finally snapped open, only the whites were showing. "Who here seeks congress with the beyond?" she asked the room. The voice was now deep and husky, with what sounded to Houdini's ears like a Russian accent. Before the séance began, the girl clearly sounded British, her voice the high pitch of a young girl. Now she practically sounded like an old woman.

"Is that you, Helena?" said Perdurabo.

"It is, Frater," answered the girl. "Now who seeks an audience with their loved ones in the beyond?"

Doyle sat back in his chair, amazed. "She's been taken over by her spirit medium!" he exclaimed.

Houdini simply watched, impressed by the showmanship on the part of Perdurabo and the young girl. He was beginning to see why this pair was so popular.

A middle aged man near the front row raised his hand. Houdini watched closely, for this could be a "plant," an acquaintance of the medium they had paid to volunteer to commune with the spirit world.

"What would you like to know?" asked Perdurabo.

"Well, it's…" the man paused, stammering for a moment. He looked as if he was embarrassed. Someone sitting next to him said something to him, and he finally spoke. "I-it's my son. He died last year. I'd just like to know if he's all right. Is he happy?"

The young girl swayed in her seat for a time, then looked straight at the man, the whites of her eyes still showing. "Your son came through briefly," she said in that thick Russian accent. "He says he is fine and very happy here in the beyond."

The man nodded and sat down, and a round of applause arose from the audience. Doyle added his clapping to the din, but Houdini and Beck didn't move.

"Who else among you seeks congress with the beyond?" the girl intoned.

One by one, people came forward. Sometimes a specific message was delivered from the other side, other times not. Sometimes the girl, under the influence of her alleged spirit medium, would make startlingly prescient comments about the people in the room, which thoroughly astounded Doyle, judging by the look on the author's face. Houdini, on the other hand, had witnessed such feats before. Doyle's own literary creation Sherlock Holmes could make equally astounding insights into people just through a combination of deductive logic and careful observation. So far the showman was unimpressed.

"I have a message from the beyond," said the girl. "A great change is coming that will affect us all. I see flames and darkness ahead. But beyond that will be a New Dawn. We must be ready. To show you that what I have seen is true, I give you a sign from the beyond."

The girl shifted in her chair as if adjusting her legs. She closed her eyes while the crowd murmured. Slowly the girl began to lift out of her chair. She wasn't standing; as she lifted above the table everyone could plainly see that her legs were crossed beneath her white gown. The girl was levitating. She rose about five feet above the table and hovered there, while the crowd let out a collective gasp of astonishment. A woman in one of the aisle seats fainted.

After hovering for a few moments, the girl lowered back into her chair and slumped forward, her head down. Frater Perdurabo once again ascended the platform and touched her head, leaned in close, and whispered something.

Soon the girl looked up, her brown eyes looking at the crowd. "Was she here?" she asked her companion.

"She was," said the man. The crowd shot to their feet and erupted in applause.

"Well?" said Doyle, leaning in close to Houdini so he could be heard over the noise. "What do you think of that?"

"I'm curious to know the answer to that myself," said Beck. "How on Earth did she do that?"

Houdini looked at the author, then at his agent, and then back at the crowd towering over them in a standing ovation. After a long moment he said, "I have no idea."

⁓ᘰ⁓

The author, the showman, and his agent waited as the crowd slowly filed out and left the large room, hoping to gain an interview with Frater Perdurabo and Miss Watson.

When most of the people had vacated the space, Houdini approached the stage, followed closely by Doyle and Beck.

Two burly men appeared from backstage to move the table. "What do you want?" the bigger of the two barked at them.

"We'd like to see Miss Watson and Frater Perdurabo," said Houdini.

"You and everyone else," grumbled the stagehand. "Get lost!"

"Well I never!" Doyle exclaimed. Houdini raised a calming hand. "How may we gain audience with them?" asked the showman. "I am, er, Joseph Adler, with the London News, and this is Sir Arthur Conan Doyle. We are doing an expose on spiritualism."

The stagehands looked at one another. The second brute said, "I don't care if you're the bloody Pope, you can't see Madam Watson or Brother Perdurabo."

"Please," said Doyle. "It's…"

"All right," said the stagehand, and he and his associate ceased their moving of the table and jumped off the stage, rolling up their sleeves. "We tried to be nice. Now it's time for you three gents to leave before someone gets hurt."

Houdini removed his fake glasses and frock coat, handing them to Beck.

"Houdini," pleaded his agent. "Perhaps we should…"

"I won't be moved by a couple of toughs," said the showman. "If it's a fight these two want, it's a fight they'll have."

The escapist backed up, raising his fists and taking a boxing stance. To his surprise, Doyle stood firm with him, raising his fists as well.

"I won't be scared away by a couple of ruffians," the author snapped. "And I shall speak to the theater owner about his hiring practices."

"We work for Madam Watson and Frater Perdurabo," said the stagehand. His associate remained eerily silent.

With that the stagehand closed on Houdini and Doyle. Beck shrieked and backed away, raising Houdini's frock coat in front of him like a shield.

Houdini let the stagehand take the first swing, a haymaker the magician easily dodged. He countered, ducking low and punching the burly oaf in the solar plexus. The stagehand went to his knees.

The portly Doyle closed with his opponent, barely moving out of the way several times before landing a few good blows to the ruffian's face, connecting solidly with his nose. There was a very audible crack as blood flowed from the man's nostrils.

"Enough!" a voice from behind them boomed. Houdini, Doyle and Beck glanced up to see the dark figure of Frater Perdurabo standing before them.

"May I help you gentlemen?" he said.

~⚬⚬⚬~

Houdini, Doyle and Beck stood in a small room just off the auditorium where they had witnessed the séance. Frater Perdurabo slouched in a chair next to Miss Watson, who sat methodically brushing her long auburn tresses and smiling like a cherub at her three visitors.

Houdini reassessed her. If he didn't know better, he would have thought her just an innocent young girl from high society, just a few short years away from blossoming into womanhood. She looked out of place next to the slouching, sneering Perdurabo, whose mere presence was enough to make the showman feel uncomfortable. Houdini sensed that Doyle and Beck could feel it too. Something about the man was palpably disagreeable.

"I must apologize for my acolytes' behavior just now," said Perdurabo. "I have enemies, and they were only trying to protect us."

"I was impressed by your séance," said Houdini.

Perdurabo and Miss Watson looked at each other and smiled. "We always strive to open one's eyes to the reality of the spiritual world all around us," said Perdurabo. "Dear Miss Watson here is a very talented medium."

The girl blushed. "I only go where the spirits lead me, Frater." She set down her hairbrush and put her hands on her lap. "I sense the skeptic in you, Mr. Houdini."

The escapist made a slight bow. "Guilty as charged, Miss Watson."

"On the other hand," put in Doyle. "I am a staunch supporter of spiritualism."

Perdurabo nodded. "Yes, Sir Arthur. And your support has not gone unnoticed."

"I was most impressed by your levitation at the end," said Houdini, changing the subject. "It was quite amazing."

The young girl blushed even more. "Did I levitate again? It is the work of the spirits."

"Actually," said Perdurabo, "one spirit in particular. Her spirit guide, Madam Helena Blavatsky."

Houdini's eyes bulged. Doyle let out a "By Jove!" Both men were familiar with the famous Russian spiritualist and mystic, now deceased for almost ten years.

"That explains the Russian accent you exhibited," said Houdini, smiling. He would have to proceed carefully now, and pretend to buy what these two were selling. At least until he figured out what their game was.

"Yes," said Perdurabo. "And the levitation, which was chief among Madam Blavatsky's many abilities in life. She has been very helpful to me, even though our paths unfortunately never crossed in this world."

"How is she helping you?" asked Doyle.

"She has warned me of a time of great sorrow not many years hence," said Perdurabo. "She is helping us get ready. Miss Watson and I are recruiting, if you will, a group of people who are open to the beyond and can be trained as clairvoyants, mediums, and ceremonial magicians to aid Britain in the coming conflict."

"It sounds like you're raising an army!" bellowed Doyle.

Perdurabo shrugged. "If you insist. The similarities with military recruitment are not lost on us. Call us psychic soldiers if you will. In fact, we have successfully recruited several high-ranking officials in the British government to our cause."

"Really?" said Doyle.

"Oh yes. When the conflict arises I want to lead the charge on the psychic front."

Houdini shook his head. "Psychic front?"

"Yes. To be successful, a war must be fought from all sides. Madam Blavatsky tells us that this war will be fought on both planes, with consequences for this world as well as the next."

"Sounds like you've got your work cut out for you," said Beck glibly.

"You are more right than you know, Mr. Beck," said Perdurabo, ignoring the agent's barb. "That's why we are channeling our efforts to retrieve a certain artifact that will assure our victory."

Houdini arched an eyebrow. "What is this artifact?"

"Are you familiar with the Spear of Destiny?"

"By Jove!" said Doyle. "You've found it?"

"Not yet. But we believe we are close."

"Spear of Destiny?" asked Houdini.

"Also known as the staff of Longinus," said Perdurabo. "It's the spear that pierced Christ's side at the Crucifixion. It is said that whoever possesses this spear shall rule the world."

"And you believe this story?" said Houdini, his patience for poppycock reaching its zenith.

Perdurabo gave a self-deprecating smile. "I am not a Christian, Mr. Houdini, but I believe this object holds some incredible power. If it were not so, Madam Blavatsky, via Miss Watson here, wouldn't have told me so."

"Interesting," said the escapist. "So where is this destiny spear?"

"We believe it is somewhere in London," said Miss Watson. "Madam Blavatsky isn't certain, for there are veils that even she cannot pierce where the Spear is concerned. But we have good reason to believe it is here."

"Would you gentlemen be interested in joining our cause?" asked Perdurabo, interrupting the girl.

"Well, I…" Doyle began, but one glance at his companion made him reconsider his words.

"We are interested in pursuing all claims of the so-called preternatural," said Houdini. "But no, until we see more evidence that what you say is real and true, we must remain interested yet passive observers."

"Interesting. So where is this destiny spear?"

Perdurabo nodded. "I understand your reticence to participate. But soon the time to remain passive will be over. People will find themselves either on the side of goodness and light, or aligned with the dark forces that threaten us all."

⌇〇⌇

"Is it just me?" Beck observed when they were outside the Egyptian Hall waiting on a carriage after Frater Perdurabo had hastily ended their meeting, "Or did that man give us all a severe case of the heebie jeebies?"

Doyle chuckled. "I'm not familiar with the term 'heebie jeebies,' but if it means to make one's skin crawl, you are correct."

"There was something very odd about him," said Houdini. "I don't believe in auras and animal magnetism, but he certainly possesses some disagreeable quality."

"Made all the worse by his history," said Doyle.

Houdini and Beck stared at the author.

"You don't know who he is, do you?"

The magician and his agent admitted that they did not.

"That was the infamous Aleister Crowley," said Doyle. "I didn't want to say anything, for fear of spooking him, if you'll pardon the obvious pun. I recognized him once I got a look at him up close."

"I've heard of this fellow," said Houdini. "He's some sort of occultist?"

Doyle nodded while Beck waived down a passing hansom. "A ceremonial magician, as he calls himself. British society has a more colorful nom de guerre for him: The Great Beast."

"I daresay he's earned that one," Houdini said as they entered the hansom cab that pulled up to the curb, followed by Doyle, then Beck, who gave the driver the address of their hotel.

"Yes," said Doyle. "He's quite the blackguard. With no regard to how a proper English gentleman should behave. I cannot believe he has managed to sway any part of the Crown to his cause."

"And what cause is that?" asked Beck. "What is this coming conflict he was going on about?"

Houdini shrugged. "It could be any number of things. Perhaps it is a reference to the political climate of Europe, or it could refer to some spiritual or metaphysical conflict. We shall have to do more digging to determine what exactly he's up to."

Beck sighed. "Am I to believe this side trip has yet to reach its destination?"

"Quite so, old friend," said Houdini. "Don't worry. The show will go on as planned."

The next morning Doyle met Houdini outside his hotel, and the two men went to interview Marjorie's brother Malcolm. Beck went to the Alhambra to make the final preparations for that evening's performance. Per Beck's suggestion, the author and the magician looked for Mortimer Blair and flagged him down. The older man was excited to see them again, and all too happy to take them wherever they wanted to go free of charge.

"Quite a display last night," said Doyle as the old dray horse, Nelly, pulled them out into traffic.

"Yes it was," Houdini replied.

"Have you figured out how the girl levitated above the crowd?"

"Not yet. But I will."

Doyle grinned. "I wish you would just accept what you have seen with your eyes. The medium's levitation could only be accomplished through supernatural means. You know that Madam Blavatsky was famous in part for levitating, and the girl channels her spirit."

"We'll see," said Houdini. "I haven't made up my mind about that yet."

Doyle grumbled something low in his throat.

"What did you learn about our friend Crowley?" asked Houdini, changing the subject.

"Well, he has traveled abroad extensively," said Doyle. Chiefly the United States, Mexico, and Egypt."

"Egypt?"

The author nodded. "That's probably where he picked up his outlandish pseudonym."

The magician chuckled. "Yes, he certainly has a penchant for the dramatic."

"As do you, my dear fellow. Though Crowley puts his dramatic flair to more sinister uses."

"How do you mean?"

"According to one of my Spiritualist colleagues, Crowley was allegedly accused of stealing an artifact from the Egyptian Museum in Cairo," explained Doyle. "I have no idea if it is true, but I am inclined to believe it, based on everything I've ever heard about the man."

"Intriguing," said Houdini. "Didn't you mention that the Pierce family has some sort of ties to Egypt?"

Their grandfather was an explorer of some note who brought back a number of artifacts," said Doyle. "You think there's some connection?"

Houdini shrugged. "That's what we must find out, old friend."

Pierce Manor was actually the Pierce family's city home they used when Marjorie or her brother were in London, a stately home on Piccadilly Circus. Mortimer Blair guided his carriage expertly to a stop in front of it, and the men got out. "I'll be in the neighborhood, so just whistle and me an' Nelly here will come runnin'," said the coachman.

The author and the magician thanked him and proceeded up to the house.

A taciturn butler answered the bell, and they were ushered into a small yet lavishly furnished sitting room. After five or ten minutes, a young man with dark hair entered the room, smiling. "My sister told me I might be receiving famous visitors. It is an honor to have you both in my home. I am Ronald Pierce."

They shook hands and exchanged pleasantries. Finally, Pierce said, "I take it you've seen Madam Watson."

"Yes," said Doyle. "Last night. Most impressive."

"Your sister is concerned for your welfare," Houdini cut in. "She believes this Ms. Watson and her companion…"

"Frater Perdurabo," Pierce interjected.

"Yes. She believes Ms. Watson and this Perdurabo to be frauds."

Pierce smiled. "My little sister worries overmuch. What do you gentlemen think?"

Doyle started to say something, but Houdini interrupted him. "I think that they are most assuredly frauds. Frater Perdurabo's real name is Aleister Crowley, a man of infamous reputation who may also be a thief. Have you given them any money?"

Pierce looked taken aback. "Not that it's any of your business, Sir, but yes, I have. Just a small fee to get into the program."

"Program?" asked Doyle.

"Yes. It's wonderful. Ms. Watson and Perdurabo help people by getting them in touch with their past lives. I don't know what Marjorie told you about me, and this is a bit embarrassing, but I have suffered from melancholia all my life. Oh, it comes and goes, but at times it can be quite debilitating. On some occasions I cannot muster the energy to get out of bed, and the condition can last for weeks. I've tried everything, and Madam Watson's sessions are the only thing that have helped."

"A past life regression?" said Doyle. "Fascinating. How is this achieved?"

"I'm not sure," said Pierce. "They put you into some sort of trance, and then you're that other person. They teach us that any difficulties we might have had in a past life can still cause us pain in the current one, if we don't work them out. These problems just keep repeating themselves over and over, you see, throughout time. Watson and Perdurabo get us in touch with our past life where the problems first began, and help our past self and us work through it."

"What person were you in this other life?" asked Doyle.

"A Roman centurion. Someone named Longinus."

Understanding dawned on Doyle's face, but Houdini shot him a look that said he should keep silent.

"Ever heard of the Spear of Destiny?"

Pierce smiled. "Every armchair archaeologist worth his salt knows that old bedtime story. My grandfather made quite a few finds in Arabia and Egypt. He used to tell me about them whenever he came home. The Destiny Spear was his favorite story."

"Did he ever find the spear?"

Pierce laughed. "Oh, this just gets better and better. No, Mr. Houdini, I don't believe my grandfather ever found it, if it existed at all."

"Crowley believes it does," said Doyle. "And he will stop at nothing to obtain it. We believe he thinks you have it."

"What? But that's absurd."

"That may be," added Houdini. "But Crowley doesn't think so. He told us he's looking for it, and why."

"Yes, the coming war or some such thing. He's spoken of it many times."

"You're not a member of his psychic army?" said Doyle

Pierce shook his head. "No. Of course not. He's merely helping me with my melancholia. I have no interest in practicing magic."

"Did Crowley seek you out, or did you contact him?"

"Why, I sought him out of course."

"Ever heard of a past life regression?" Houdini asked the author.

"No. I'm usually so up to date when it comes to spiritualist affairs, but I've heard nothing of this form of psychic treatment."

"It is completely new, so I'm given to understand," said Pierce. "Madam Watson told me that Frater Perdurabo brought it from Egypt. So, gentlemen, I'm afraid this is nothing more than my dear sister living in fear of me frittering away her share of the inheritance. But not to worry. I have no intention of handing over my entire estate to Frater and Ms. Watson. But they are helping me immeasurably, and I don't need or want any help from my sister or you."

"Mesmeric trances are nothing new," said Houdini to Doyle, as if ignoring Pierce.

"That's true," said Doyle. "Forty years ago they were all the rage, but they had nothing to do with past lives, spirits or levitation."

"Are you gentlemen not listening to me?" Pierce said, agitated. "I'm afraid I must ask you to leave."

The butler appeared to see them out.

"Wait, please," said Houdini. "May we try something? With Doyle's assistance, I'd like to put you in another trance similar to the one Ms. Watson and her companion put you under."

"Of course," said Doyle. "I'm somewhat of a mesmerist myself."

Pierce looked at them for a long moment, then shooed his butler away. "Fine. If it will get my sister off my back, and you two off my property."

They had Pierce lie down on the leather sofa in his parlor. Doyle pulled over an ottoman to sit close beside him while Houdini stood at the foot of the sofa. The author began by getting Pierce to relax, taking deep breaths with him while he went through the process of placing his fingers near Pierce's face in different areas in a procedure known as mesmeric touching. Houdini watched patiently as Pierce was slowly placed into a trance.

"He's under," Doyle whispered to Houdini when he was finished. "He went quickly too. He's either very susceptible to mesmeric suggestion, or his mind has undergone it numerous times. What do you want to do next?"

"I want to know what they did to him while he was mesmerized before," said Houdini. "Ask him to recall those memories and sensations."

"I want you to think back to your first session with Madam Watson and Frater Perduabo," Doyle said softly. "Can you see it?"

"Yes," said Pierce.

"Good. I want you to remember everything about that session with perfect clarity. Tell me what happened."

"I am standing on the banks of a narrow stream, looking down into the water. I can see my reflection, as well as the reflections of others staring back at me. Sister Watson tells me these are the people I was in the past, and the stream itself is Time, flowing ever so steadily into the future. I can see men and women staring back at me, smiling as if they recognize me, and in a moment I recognize them. Their names, their deeds, all come rushing back to me like forgotten memories. She tells me to lean closer and I become them, all of them, all at once."

"Then what happened? Can you recall a specific moment?"

"Ask him about he spear," said Houdini.

"Can you see the spear?" Doyle asked Pierce.

Pierce turned his head left and right quickly, as if struggling with something. "Yes. I see it."

"Describe everything you see," said Doyle.

"He is holding it. Longinus is holding it. It is dripping with blood. The blood of the man who proclaimed himself King of the Jews."

"But you are Longinus," said Doyle, perplexed.

Pierce shook his head. "No. I am Octavius, loyal page of noble Longinus. He hands the spear to me, tells me to keep it safe. He fears the Jews will try to steal it, make it into a holy relic."

Doyle and Houdini locked eyes with one another.

"I am protector of the spear," said Pierce. "All throughout time."

"Where is Longinus?" asked Houdini.

"Longinus is with me always," said Pierce. "We are bound together by blood and time."

"Good Lord," Doyle said to Houdini. "You don't think..?"

"That Marjorie Pierce is Longinus?" said Houdini. It would appear our friend Crowley thinks so, and might be using her brother to get to her. She doesn't trust Crowley one bit, and would never go to him unbidden for any reason."

"Ms. Pierce could be in great danger," said Doyle. "I wouldn't put anything past The Great Beast."

At the mention of Crowley's nickname, Pierce cried out and began to thrash on the couch. Houdini moved to hold him down while Doyle quickly brought him out of the trance. "You will remember nothing that has transpired," he told Pierce.

The man calmed down and, a few seconds later, opened his eyes. "Well?" he asked, looking at the two men, who were at this point leaning over him.

"I think we got what we came for," said Houdini. "We're sorry to have troubled you, Mr. Pierce. We'll see ourselves out."

Houdini grabbed Doyle by the arm before he could protest, and half dragged the older, taller man out the front door.

"What now, Houdini?"

"We must find Ms. Pierce at once, old friend. As soon as Crowley can get his hands on her, I'm certain he'll do so, believing she'll lead him directly to the spear."

"We must not let an artifact that powerful fall into the hands of a man like Crowley," said Doyle.

Houdini shrugged. "For the moment, I am more concerned with Ms. Pierce's safety. Let's go!"

Mortimer Blair was still in the area, and he had circled back round to meet Houdini and Doyle just as they were ready to put Pierce Manor behind them. After a quick stop by the Alhambra to give a message to Beck, Houdini gave their coachman the address of Marjorie Pierce's city home.

"Do you think we can reach the poor girl in time?" said Doyle after they climbed into the carriage.

"I certainly hope so," said Houdini.

Doyle smiled, checking his pocket watch. "I knew I could count on you, Houdini! Who better to foil a magician than another magician."

"Don't congratulate me just yet, dear fellow. Not until we've called on Ms. Pierce and gotten her some police protection."

Houdini looked to his left at the London traffic moving past the carriage. "As for Ms. Watson's channeling of the deceased Madam Blavatsky, and her seemingly miraculous levitation, I believe I have the answer to that little mystery."

"Oh, do tell!"

"In good time, Doyle. In good time."

When they arrived at Ms. Pierce's city estate, a quaint though well-appointed cottage style abode, Houdini and Doyle found the front door standing wide open, and the place torn apart by a struggle.

A disheveled cook named Ms. Hedwig was on the floor on her hands and knees, sobbing and picking up pieces of broken china. Houdini asked her what happened.

"Oh dearest me," she groaned. These two bullish men came in and took Ms. Marjorie. Oh, it'll be the devil when she finds they broke her grandmother's china!"

Houdini gripped her shoulders and shook her. "Have you called the police?"

Ms. Hedwig looked at Houdini as if she was squinting at him from across a great distance. "What? No. Ms. Marjorie wouldn't want 'em to see such a mess!"

"I think she's in shock," said Doyle. "I'll look for the phone."

The author left the room and came back a few minutes later. "I rang Scotland Yard and told my old friend Milton Sedgewick what happened. He's sending some men."

"Good," said Houdini. "Though he should have sent some men sooner."

"What do we do now?"

Houdini helped the cook to her feet and into a chair. "Now we go get Marjorie Pierce. Fortunately, I know exactly where Crowley is keeping her."

⚯

"Shouldn't we await the police?" Doyle asked as Mortimer Blair's carriage pulled up to the house they had visited yesterday.

"There may not be enough time," said Houdini. "We've given them the address, so they will arrive momentarily."

Houdini climbed down from the carriage. "You gents be careful," said Blair, a look of grave concern on his face.

Doyle got down and looked up at the coachman. "Please go and find the first policeman you come across."

Blair gave a little salute. "Will do, Sir Arthur, sir. Good luck and Godspeed."

With that he was off, his dray clomping up the street. The showman and the author were alone in front of the house.

"Looks like no one's home," said Doyle.

"They'll be in the basement I suspect," said Houdini. "I'm sure our friend Crowley feels some ritual is in order to glean the location of the Destiny Spear."

"That horrible man," grumbled Doyle. "Let's get in there and put this to rights."

Houdini grinned. "I thought you'd never ask."

The front door was, of course, locked, so Houdini produced a set of lockpicks from his sleeve and went to work. In mere moments, the door popped open and they cautiously went inside.

The foyer was dark, and no one appeared to be about. "Listen," said Houdini. Do you hear it?"

Doyle cocked his head. "Yes. I think I do. It's a low chanting."

"Yes," said the handcuff king. "The basement!"

The author followed the showman deeper into the house, looking for a door that might lead to the basement. Finding none, Houdini began tapping the walls.

"If this home is used for séances, it's bound to have secret doors or passageways," said Houdini.

Doyle tested a section of wall with his hand. "Just because we're in the home of a spiritualist doesn't mean—ahh!"

Houdini turned just as Doyle was falling into an opening in the wall behind him. He ran to where his friend had stood seconds before, watching as the panel sprang back into place. Houdini began touching it, pushing on it with all his weight. Finally he placed his palm on a section of wall at about Doyle's height, and watched as the door clicked open. It was on some sort of spring, and wanted to snap back, but Houdini pushed it open further and cautiously entered the darkness beyond. He took one step and suddenly found himself falling straight down.

All around him was darkness. A musty smell met his nostrils. Slowly, cautiously, the showman pulled himself up to his knees and stood. He patted himself, checking for cuts or broken bones. He was in one piece, but he knew he'd be sore the next day.

Suddenly, a black sack was thrust over his head, and rough hands seized him, dragging farther into the gloom. At first he resisted, then he realized they were probably taking him to Doyle and Ms. Pierce, which was precisely where he wanted to go.

Houdini heard the men holding him grumbling and snickering, and recognized the voices as belonging to Crowley's thuggish stagehands who had accosted them that afternoon.

The escapist was thrown into a wooden chair and hastily tied up, the black sack removed from his head.

"Check his pockets," said one. "He's a professional escape artist, and no doubt conceals many such tools of that trade on his person. Search him good."

As the brutes patted Houdini, digging into his pockets, the showman looked at his surroundings. He was in a large chamber that appeared to be part of London's sewer system. Below him was a large, high-walled basin. Doyle and Ms. Pierce were tied to chairs in the middle of this basin, and a large pipe jutted from the brick wall opposite them and Houdini.

"What is the meaning of this?" asked the escapist. "Untie us at once."

"All in due time, Houdini."

Houdini craned his neck. Atop the wall opposite them stood Crowley, resplendent in a flowing crimson robe. Miss Watson stood beside him in glowing white.

When the stagehands were through securing Houdini, one of them climbed down a set of iron rungs set in the wall of the basin and removed the sacks from Doyle and Ms. Pierce. They looked around, blinking.

"I say, Houdini!" yelled Doyle. "What is going on here?"

Houdini produced a set of lockpicks from his sleeve and went to work.

"I was just getting to that," said Crowley. "Houdini, the famous magician, is going to perform for us tonight. He is going to retrieve the Spear of Destiny for us."

"What are you talking about?" said Doyle. "Untie us, you blackguard!" Behind them, Ms. Pierce whimpered and wept softly.

"Moments ago, Ms. Pierce kindly revealed the current location of the Spear," Crowley said. "It was in her possession for several years, a gift from her archaeologist grandfather. But not knowing what it was, she gave it, along with her grandfather's other trinkets, to the British Museum."

"What does that have to do with me?" said Houdini.

Crowley's eyes narrowed to slits. "You are going to break into the museum tonight and retrieve the Spear for me."

"And if I refuse?"

Crowley nodded to one of his thugs, who started turning a wheel set in the far wall, above the basin. The pipe jutting from the wall of the basin began trickling water. Then it became a stream, then a torrent.

"The water will be over their heads in about three hours," said Crowley. "I suggest you get started."

One of Crowley's men cut Houdini loose with a sharp knife, even though he was almost free of his bonds. "What's to keep me from going to the police and sending them straight here?"

"You don't know where 'here' is," said Crowley. "You shall be led out of here blind. When you have the Spear, return to the house, and someone will lead you down the way you barged in the first time around."

"Put this on," said one of Crowley's thugs, pointing a gun at him and tossing at him the black sack that had been placed over his head earlier.

Houdini obediently placed the sack over his head, then the stagehand poked the showman in the ribs with the gun barrel and, gripping his elbow, started walking. Houdini was led up and out of the tunnel system as he tried not to concentrate on the sounds of rushing water and the protests of Crowley's captives behind him.

One he was outside, Crowley's thug ripped the sack from his head. Houdini looked around, blinking. They were not near the house at all, but in some sort of wooded area. It was now early evening, and dark beneath the trees where they stood. The entrance to the sewers, he knew, must be somewhere around him, but where? Crowley was right. He would never find it, and any police search of the tunnels under the house might lead them to Doyle and Ms. Pierce after it was already too late. Whatever he did now, he would have to do it quickly.

"I suggest you find your way to the British Museum," said the thug. "And hop to it. When you have the Spear, return to the house. Someone will let you in, and we'll release your friends."

"And if I refuse?"

"The clock is ticking, guvnor." With that he vanished into the shadows.

Houdini grumbled in frustration. He didn't have time to pursue; he would just be fumbling around in the dark. He headed instead for the distant glow of gas lamps, and what would hopefully be a street. Just as he cleared the tangle of trees, he heard the familiar clomp of heavy hooves.

"Well! Halloo there, Mr. Houdini, Sir. What brings you all the way out 'ere this fine evenin'?"

"Hello, Morty," said the showman. "I'm afraid I don't have much time to explain. Can you get me to the British Museum?"

"Well, sure. But the museum'll be closin' up soon."

"We'd best hurry, then."

"Climb on up. Nelly'll get us there if I have to get out and help her pull meself! On, Nelly! Or it's straight to the glue fac'try! Giddyup!"

No sooner had Houdini climbed aboard than the old dray trotted off, her hooves clapping against the cobblestones.

Houdini quickly weighed his options. Wherever Doyle and Ms. Pierce were being held, it was far from Crowley's home, in a maze of underground tunnels. The police would never reach them in time. If he showed up at the house empty handed, they would all surely be killed. Whatever he did, and he had no intention of breaking into the British Museum and stealing some priceless artifact, he would have to do now.

Slowly, a plan began to form in the showman's brain.

"Morty," said Houdini. "On the way to the museum, stop by the first policeman we pass. I'd like to have a word with him."

"Yes Sir!"

They had almost reached the museum by the time they spotted anyone in uniform. Mortimer Blair stopped his carriage, and Houdini got out to explain his wild plan to the rather confused but compliant policeman.

An hour later, a harried Houdini banged incessantly on the door of Crowley's home. Finally the gaslights came on and the door opened to reveal a sour-faced butler. "He's been expecting you, sir. Follow me."

The butler lead Houdini to the wall where he and Doyle had fallen through into the underground lair of Aleister Crowley. "Do you have the item?" asked the butler.

"Right here," said the handcuff king, gesturing to a long pointy shape wrapped in red velvet clutched in his right hand.

"Very good."

The butler tapped a spot on the wall, and it swung open. The space was now well lit by gas lamps.

Houdini turned. The butler had vanished. Grinning, Houdini ducked into the hole in the wall and was gone.

Houdini knew he was close when the sound of rushing water filled his ears. Doyle and Ms. Pierce still sat in the center of the basin, the water almost to their shoulders.

"Houdini!" sputtered Doyle. "You're back!"

"Yes," said the showman proudly. "And I'm not empty-handed. Where's that blackguard Crowley?"

"Right here."

Houdini looked. Standing on the other side of the basin was Crowley, young Miss Watson standing by his side. "Did you acquire the Spear?"

"I did," said Houdini. And I'll give it to you once you turn off that water and drain the basin."

"First let me see it," said Crowley.

"First drain the basin," countered Houdini.

Crowley considered this for a long moment. Finally, he gave a flick of his wrist to one of his cruel stagehands, and the water slowly stopped. Then, a moment later, the basin started to drain.

"Such an old thing," said Houdini. "I still do not know what all the fuss is about."

"Nevertheless. Give it to us."

"Please, Mr. Houdini," said Miss Watson. "You're making Frater terribly cross. Just give him what we want and you and your friends may leave. They only want the Spear."

"You mean Crowley and Madam Blavatsky," said Houdini.

Miss Watson scowled. "If she were here, she'd take it from you! She's quite powerful, you know."

Houdini chuckled. "Oh yes, I saw her little demonstration. Very well. Come and take it."

"We don't have time for this nonsense!" grumbled Crowley, and he bounded from his place beside the girl and ran over to where Houdini stood, his robes flowing ghostlike around him.

"Give it here!"

"Certainly," said the showman, and lifted the piece of fabric.

Crowley reached for it greedily. Just as his hands closed upon it, Houdini threw back the velvet and clapped a pair of handcuffs around the Great Beast's wrists.

"What is this?" Crowley hissed.

"Just a little trick between magicians."

"You'll pay for this, Houdini. Or rather, your friends will. Fetch! Gimble! Kill them. Kill them all!"

In the shadows behind Miss Watson they heard a scuffling and raised voices. Two policemen appeared with Crowley's stagehands Fetch and Gimble in cuffs.

"What?" said Crowley.

Houdini gave a playful shrug. "I tried as best I could, but they followed me back here." He lifted his left foot and indicated the bottom of his shoe. "Must be all this glow-in-the-dark paint I stepped in."

Crowley peered over Houdini's shoulder and saw a set of glowing footprints going back the way the escapist had come.

"Once I told the police where your lackey had lead me out, and I described where Doyle and Miss Pierce were being held, they knew exactly where it was and found a shortcut. This place is surrounded by police, as is the house above."

"But," sputtered Crowley. "The Spear!"

"I also had a little chat with the curator of the British Museum," said Houdini. "Nothing matching the Spear's description has ever been in their possession. I'm afraid your Spear of Destiny is lost to time, if it ever existed at all."

Crowley was still sputtering incoherently when the police carted him off. Houdini descended into the basin to help free Doyle and Miss Pierce, who were both soaking wet but glad to be alive.

"Very good, Houdini," said Doyle as Houdini untied him. "I was afraid there was no escape."

"There's always an escape," said Houdini. "If you know where to look. Thankfully I had some assistance with this trick." Houdini looked up at one of the policemen and gave him a wink.

Doyle followed his gaze. "Who is that? I say!"

A familiar face melted out of the shadows and climbed down the rungs into the soggy basin. "Hello, Sir Arthur. Very nice to meet you. I'm a big admirer of your work. Reginald Mortimer of Scotland Yard, at your service." He did a little bow. "My friends call me Morty."

"Why, it's Mortimer Blair, our coachman!" Doyle leaped from his chair as soon as he was free and shook Mortimer's hand.

"I was working incognito," said Mortimer, every trace of his cockney accent gone. "I work for a special agency attached to the Crown. Crowley was suspected of being a threat to England, and I've been on his tail for months. I figured you two would run into him once you got involved in the Pierce family's, uh, predicament, and knew you'd need a hand."

Doyle smiled. "That's why you were always right there whenever we needed a lift."

"Precisely," said Morty. "I was following you, thinking you'd lead me right to Crowley. He's been able to spot the police a mile away and has steered clear of them. The Crown owes you both a debt of thanks."

"As do I," said Ms. Pierce. "I don't know how to repay you."

"Just get me out of here and into some dry clothes," said Doyle. "And any debt you think you owe me is paid in full!"

They all laughed as Morty lead them out of the tunnels and back into more familiar environs.

⤷꧁꧂↶

Houdini invited Doyle and Miss Pierce to his final show in London, which was a rousing success. Beck managed to parlay Houdini's adventures around the city into a media spectacle, which no doubt helped fill a few more seats at the Alhambra than they might have otherwise.

Houdini, Doyle and Beck had to sneak out the back of the theater to deafening applause once the show was over.

"I wonder what will happen to Crowley and Miss Watson," Houdini mused as they headed for Houdini's motorcar that would take he and Beck to the harbor.

"He has money and connections," said Doyle. "I suppose a mere slap on the wrist, even though I'll do my best to make sure they don't overlook his kidnapping and near drowning of two innocent people. As for Miss Watson, I hear she's already been shipped off home to her parents in Somerset or thereabouts. She'll remain there in quiet seclusion until this whole thing dies down. It's a shame too, as I feel she is a legitimate medium."

"What about Miss Watson's levitation?" asked Beck.

"Simple," said Houdini. "A wire and pulley system operated by Crowley's two stagehands."

"You don't know that for a fact," said Doyle. "I saw no wires."

"Nor did I," countered the showman. "But as you are so fond of pointing out, just because one cannot see a thing, doesn't mean it isn't there."

Doyle scowled and said nothing, while Beck simply grinned and shook his head. It would always be this way for these two friends.

"What's next for you, then?" said Doyle, changing the subject.

"Paris," said Houdini. "And another performance."

"And no more adventures," added Beck.

Doyle shook hands with the two men. "I think you will find that life itself is quite an adventure."

Houdini smiled and nodded. That was definitely something the two of them could agree on.

THE END

HOUDINI AND THE GRAIN OF TRUTH

When Ron Fortier announced that he was putting together a pulp anthology featuring the great Harry Houdini, I couldn't *not* offer up a story. But seconds after I hit 'Send' on the email stating my intent to contribute, I had a momentary bout of writer's panic. What was I going to write about?

I knew some of the other contributors were pairing Houdini with various historical personages, so I quickly latched upon the idea of teaming Houdini with Sir Arthur Conan Doyle. It was a no-brainer; after all, the two had been friends in real life. They had also battled over the legitimacy of Spiritualism, that nineteenth century pop religion that had spread through Europe and America in the decades following World War I, of which Doyle was its most ardent proponent, and Houdini its most vocal critic.

I then had two elements for my tale. Houdini and the recently knighted Doyle must team up and have an adventure that had something to do with Spiritualism. Already the scenario was rife with conflict, and I hadn't even started writing! But how do I ramp things up?

The answer was simple. Since Houdini and Doyle had really lived, I needed to pair them with a villain who had also really existed, and since I was dealing with Spiritualism and mediums delivering messages from beyond the grave, I quickly latched upon a "real" medium, the Russian mystic and founder of The Theosophical Society, Madam Helena Blavatsky. A quick Internet search revealed she was dead at the time I must set my tale to fit in with Captain Ron's guidelines. "No problem!" I told myself. "She can visit the story from beyond the grave!"

Once I had Madam Blavatsky "supposedly" pulling strings from the other side, it was almost natural to throw Aleister Crowley into the mix. Crowley was an English occultist, mystic, ceremonial magician and social critic who went against the basic tenets of society and was named "the wickedest man in the world."

I had my hero and his "sidekick." I also had my villains. Now all I needed was a quest or challenge. I quickly found it in the popular legend of the Spear of Destiny, the spear that pierced Christ's side at the Crucifixion and smeared in His blood. The legend also states that whoever holds the Spear shall control the world.

It was getting easier and easier for me to connect the dots, though the actual chain of events wouldn't come until much later, and there were a few false starts. There's a popular story about how Crowley went to the British government during World War II and offered to help fight the war using occult means. They said no, but the writer in me wonders how things would have gone if they'd said yes. But with this knowledge, I soon latched onto the notion that Crowley, being warned of the second war's coming by the spirit of Blavatsky communicating through a young girl, realizes that the only way for Britain to ensure victory is by him getting his hands on the Spear of Destiny, and he'll go to any means to do so.

So in putting together this story, I not only had a great amount of fun, but I was continually reminded of the adage that truth is stranger than fiction.

JAMES PALMER - has written for Pro Se Productions, Altus Press, and White Rocket Books. His work has appeared in *Gideon Cain: Demon Hunter, Blackthorn: Thunder on Mars, Mars McCoy: Volume 2* and *Tales of the Rook: Volume 2*. James is also editor and publisher of Mechanoid Press, a small press imprint devoted to science fiction and New Pulp books, anthologies, and e-books. Their first anthology is *Monster Earth*, a collection of original giant monster tales co-edited with Jim Beard.

James is author of the e-books *Slow Djinn* and *Four Terrors: Weird Horror Tales*. He blogs for the revived science fiction magazine *Amazing Stories*. A recovering comic book addict, James lives in Northeast Georgia with his wife and daughter. For more, visit www.jamespalmerbooks.com and www.mechanoidpress.com.

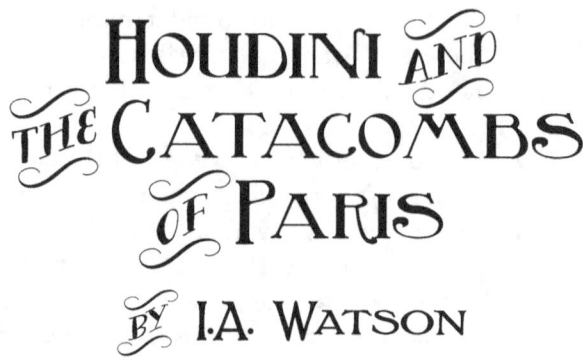

HOUDINI AND THE CATACOMBS OF PARIS

BY I.A. WATSON

"Lunatic that you are, why do you promise yourself long life, you who cannot count on a single day?"
—Inscription in the Parisian catacombs

Houdini hung upside down in a sealed burlap sack three hundred and sixty feet above the ground, swinging from the second platform of the Eiffel Tower. His hands and feet were cuffed together with Hyatt Derby patent shackles that had been additionally sealed with wax by the Mayor of Paris.[1] As an additional precaution the escape artist had been strip-searched by four officers of the 8e Regiment de Hussars before being enclosed in his dangling bag.

Close to eight thousand Parisians gathered on the World's Fair showground below to watch what Houdini would do next.

The escape artist took his time. The cross-winds were fierce and unpredictable beneath the four curving legs of the world's tallest building. His sack spun in a dizzying, irregular manner, making it difficult to concentrate. He forced himself to breathe slowly and calmly and to focus on the job at hand.

First the handcuffs had to go. The Hyatt Derbys were a well-known brand, recently favoured by the French police, but hardly impossible to beat with the right equipment. Houdini regurgitated the skeleton key he'd

---

1   For ease of narrative our story uses this title as one with which readers will be familiar. In actuality, Paris had no Mayor from 1871 to 1977. The responsibilities normally carried out by a Mayor in other French cities were divided between the Prefect of Île-de-France (who effectively served as Mayor) and a Prefect of Police covering Paris and three suburban departments. For clarity the terms Mayor and Police Prefect are used herein.

swallowed earlier – he had the trick of holding small objects in his gullet – and delicately turned the locks of the metal restraints.

Once his hands and feet were free the next problem was the thick sacking around him. The padlocks that sealed it shut were on the outside. Working by touch in the absolute darkness of the bag, Houdini dismantled the handcuffs. When the mechanism came apart his fingers sought and found the tiny sharp plates inside. The tumbler flats were keen enough to slice a fist-long hole in the top of the sack so he could reach the first of the outer locks.

A shout from someone in the crowd below alerted the rest that the showman's hand had emerged from the sack. A cheer rose up.

Houdini found the first padlock, despite swinging like a pendulum under the second platform of Gustave Eiffel's remarkable construction. The tumblers yielded to the escapologist's expert touch. The shackle spring out.

That meant the top of the bag could be part-opened. Houdini struggled an arm and his head out of the cloying burlap. The shouts and cheers of the audience grew louder. Houdini could see rows of schoolchildren down below in their Sunday best waving tiny flags, a row of carriages where the rich and powerful watched his remarkable publicity stunt through opera glasses, the seething mass of ordinary people who had turned out by the thousands to see him take on this challenge. He gave them a wave.

The other two padlocks yielded easily and Houdini was free. The bucking sack still swayed and spun under the tower's span but by the terms of his agreement all he had to do was to stretch out and seize the tricolour ribbon an arm's reach up the chain from which he dangled. He grabbed the cloth and held it up for the crowd to see.

Then he waited for Martin Beck to have him hauled up.

⁓ 𝔬𝔵𝔬 ⁓

"Mr Harry Houdini is the world's foremost expert in the science of escapology," Mr Beck instructed reporters. The entrepreneurial agent stood in one of the three great cafés of the Eiffel Tower, positioned so that the flash-pan photographs would include the span where his principal had performed and the whole Parisian skyline beyond. Without even realising it the round-faced manager had placed a hand on his lapel, assuming an almost Napoleonic pose for the pressmen. "He has no fear of heights. He first debuted on the high wire at nine years old as 'The Prince of the Air'. Since that time he has dared many feats which would make lesser men tremble at the thought of falling to their ruin!"

"Mr Houdini has performed in England to great success," one of the reporters noted.

Beck glanced over to the knot of dignitaries that swarmed around the great man. The Mayor of Paris was exclaiming how very extraordinary Houdini's escape had been. The Prefect of Police was inspecting the dismantled handcuffs with a dissatisfied glare.

"Houdini performed in London's prestigious Alhambra Theatre at the request of the great showman Mr Dundas Slater. The city was astonished at his feats of skill and daring – as your excellent Paris newspapers have reported."

"Will Monsieur Houdini be opening a show in France?"

"That is Mr Houdini's intent. He believes that the discriminating and perspicacious people of Paris will truly appreciate the wonders of his performance. We are now in negotiations with a major theatrical figure to open with a show that will make even Houdini's English performances pale into insignificance."

That provoked a new round of excited questions from the press, Beck was gratified to see. So far the escape challenge publicity stunt had never failed to ensure that Harry Houdini's arrival in any metropolis was front page news.

Another reporter came in on a different tack. "Monsieur Houdini is more than just the showman though, yes? There were reports during his time in England, events of a more sinister nature...?"

"You are not referring to Houdini's accomplishments as a card magician or illusionist, I take it," Beck acknowledged. "It is true that Houdini is a man of curious mind – how else could he succeed in challenges that make his so-called rivals despair? Sometimes when he has encountered mystery and injustice he has responded as any man of vigorous morals and superior intellect must. He has acted!"

Across the room, a sallow-faced man with a goatee was heading towards Houdini and the cluster of civic dignitaries. Beck spotted the danger and deftly detached himself from the newspapermen. "Now, *mes amis*, you must excuse me. My assistants will be happy to give you copies of Mr Houdini's extraordinary curriculum vitae, complete with photographs and engravings of his most significant accomplishments, and to answer any further questions you might have. I see a... business acquaintance with whom I must confer."

It was telling of the spell that Houdini had worked upon the usually voracious Parisian press that they were so easily handed off to Beck's subordinates. The manager was able to slide past them and intercept the sallow Frenchman before he could reach Houdini and the Mayor.

"Monsieur Lascalle," Beck greeted the *avocat*. "I trust you enjoyed the performance?"

"It was most impressive, Monsieur Beck," Lascalle replied in cultured English. If he was irritated to be blocked by Houdini's manager he succeeded in hiding it. "It has made my employer only more determined to secure your client's attention upon the challenge he has issued."

Beck smiled insincerely. In every new city there were always a dozen or more offers from people in society eager to bask in the reflected glory of some bizarre exploit they hoped Houdini would perform for them. Part of an agent's job was to protect his artiste from that press of offers. "Houdini's policy on such matters is consistent, Monsieur Lascalle. He is quite willing to consider all exploits, but insists that such challenges take place in a public forum open to general view."

"That is perhaps appropriate in England, where the masses flock and stare at every occasion, or in *les Etats-Unis d'Amérique*," the lawyer attempted not to sneer at the mention of that distant and gauche former colony, "but in Europe, and most of all in Paris its glittering centre, it is the custom of discerning men of culture and taste to gather away from the chattering mob and take their entertainments privately."

Beck knew what Lascalle wanted. "I'm afraid the Marquis will have to flock with the masses on this occasion," the manager apologised. "Houdini likes the 'chattering mob'. It is, as you say, the American way. He has declined many private performances, insisting that these tests be imposed in public meeting halls before substantial crowds."

"Perhaps we should discuss a fee?" Lascalle offered.

"It is not a matter of money. It is Houdini's policy. Please convey his regret to Monsieur le Marquis and extend Houdini's personal invitation to the opening gala night of our forthcoming show."

Lascalle's face showed some sign of emotion for the first time; disbelief or rage. "Le Marquis Etienne-Louis Pierre-Phillipe Saint Jealle de Confontaine et Asnières-de-la-Châtaigneraye is not accustomed to being denied."

"On this occasion he will have to be content with it," Beck told the lawyer. "You'll have to pardon me now. I see the Mayor is waiting for a word."

Lascalle sniffed as if to dismiss the trivial bureaucrats that clung to their petty power and privileges. "Good day, then, Monsieur Beck." He spun on his heel and headed for the elevator.

Beck retreated to join Houdini. The crowd was thinning now the food was being served. The French might appreciate a daring and unprecedented escape show; they appreciated fine cuisine even more.

"Lascalle is persistent on behalf of his Marquis, then," Houdini observed to his managing agent.

"The usual stuff. His boss has some special box of tricks he thinks would keep you baffled. Wants a private show for him and his cronies in some fancy mansion somewhere on the Left Bank. Isn't interested in dragging the contraption to a Montmartre playhouse for the proles to share."

Houdini patted his friend on the shoulder. "I owe you for throwing yourself in front of him like that."

"Just doing my job. Besides, that attorney gives me the creeps. I naturally distrust anyone who comes to see me with a contract already in his pocket."

"That's what you did to me in a Minnesota beer hall," Houdini recalled.

"And I know what I'm like – so I'm wary of others like it!" the agent chuckled.

"It's worked out fine so far. And here we are in the glamorous…" Houdini broke off in mid sentence and grabbed Beck warningly by the collar.

"What?" the manager asked, puzzled.

"Quietly. Look up there, out of the window. Right up on the crossbeam where my rope was hanging."

Beck tried to stay discreet. Everyone else was concerned with lunch, so nobody had spotted that a man had climbed out along the exposed girder and was staring at the ground three hundred and eighty feet below.

"That's not one of our workmen," Beck breathed uneasily.

"And he's not admiring the view," Houdini replied. "Cover for me, Beck."

The manager winced. "You're not going out there, are you?" He saw Houdini's set jaw and sighed. "Of course you are. Well be careful. Don't die. It would ruin the tour."

Houdini nodded acknowledgement and slipped away to return to the second platform crossbeam.[2]

~∂§⌒

---

2   The Eiffel Tower has four platforms at 186ft, 380 ft, 644ft, and 874ft. It's total height is 984ft. A leap from any of the platforms is usually fatal. One of only two survivors was a young woman whom the winds blew aside to land on a car; she subsequently recovered and married the vehicle's owner. An average of four people a year kill themselves at the Eiffel Tower, making it the third most popular form of suicide in France after poisoning and hanging.

Richard Sheffield was a desperate young man in his early twenties. He wore no coat or jacket and his collar was loose. He balanced on the narrow girder where a temporary platform had been rigged to hang Houdini's harness. The sharp wind tugged at his shirt-sleeves.

He stared at the ground below and clenched his fists.

"Looking down's always a bad idea," Houdini told him.

Sheffield hadn't heard the famous showman approach. He took a step back and almost overbalanced.

"Steady," Houdini told him. "The cross-winds up here are bad enough. Better come back inside with me. Have a glass of champagne and tell me your troubles."

Sheffield shook his head. "All the drink in the world won't solve my problems. In fact it helped cause them."

Houdini nodded. "It's been known. So what brings you here to spoil my Paris debut?"

Sheffield seemed to recognise the man who'd joined him on the high beam. "Harry Houdini!"

"The same. And you are...?"

The young man was well brought up in polite British society. "Richard Sheffield," he replied automatically. He almost held his hand out to shake before he remembered how absurd that would be given the location and circumstances. "It's no use," he added.

"Try me," Houdini offered. "I'm a good listener. At least sit down and tell me why a young Englishman's balancing on a high beam above the city of Paris, presumably gathering up the nerve to splatter himself across the pavement below."

Sheffield glanced down again. He swallowed hard. He reluctantly lowered himself to sit with his legs hanging over the Tower's support girders.

Houdini sat down with him, careful not to crowd the young man.

"I'm a fool," Sheffield said at last. "The world's biggest fool."

"That's quite a thing," Houdini replied, "given all the competition."

Sheffield snorted. "But I am. I thought I was so clever when I came out here, came to Paris to make my name. Everyone comes here, if they want to be somebody, to be part of the Bohemian revolution."

"And you wanted to... revolt?"

"I wanted to be here! To follow in the steps of Brissaud and Jarry, Matisse, Renoir, Degas! To walk the same streets of Montmartre and Montparnasse as the great Henri Marie Raymond de Toulouse-Lautrec-Monfa!"

"You wanted to paint," Houdini surmised.

"I wanted to live!" Sheffield exclaimed. "You have to understand. I wanted to break free from the shackles of social convention and express the things inside of me! I wanted... art, music, theatre, literature, all the manifestations of love!"

Houdini recognised an idealistic and naïve young man a long way from home. "So you came to Paris," he prompted.

"I escaped to Paris. I fled. And then I came to this city – this wonderful, terrible city of lights! I came to Paris and I lived!"

Houdini had to admit to himself that *fin de siècle* Paris was certainly the place to come if one wanted life in its undistilled glory. From the heights of the Tower one could see the whole Seine river basin and the hills surrounding it, the twenty *arrondissements* with their 2.7 million inhabitants. The city liked to call itself the capital of Europe. With its vibrant modern industry, its art and culture, its vast extremes of wealth and poverty, it was indeed the embodiment of the new century.

Sheffield was committed to his narrative now. "I'd been here three months before I met Le Saphir Mortel. It was she who changed my world."

"The deadly sapphire," Houdini translated. "Not her birth-name, I'd guess."

"No. She was once Marie-Anne Legris, when she first emerged from the poverty of the streets to become an actress and the muse of Montmartre."

A broken heart, then, after some unfortunate encounter with one of Paris' dazzling courtesans? "You fell for this Sapphire?"

"Of course. Who did not? And she allowed me into her inner circle, that band of brilliant minds and wits that stand at the very nadir of our new age. I painted her and they saw my talents. I was accepted amongst them, as one of their own."

"Did you come to Paris with money?" Houdini asked practically.

"No. I left everything behind, you understand. It was Le Saphir's friends who supported me, encouraged me, introduced me where it counted. It was they who first brought me to the *Club de Bord Lointain*."

"The Far Edge Club," Houdini interpreted.

"Yes. Men who believe that life can only truly be experienced when it is on the brink of extinction. Men who seek the thrill of danger to drink deep of the wine of life!"

Houdini had some sympathy for that outlook, but he knew something must have happened to bring the young man to a crossbeam of the world's tallest structure. "Did you join this Club of excitement-seeking bon-vivants?" he wondered.

"I could not. They are all rich men, very rich, able to travel across the globe in search of their adventures. Just now they are in Paris, and here I was caught up in their glittering society." Sheffield looked away. "What a fool I was!"

"Paris is made for fools," Houdini advised. "Young men come here and make mistakes. If they're fortunate they return home wiser and poorer and use what they've learned not to go wrong again."

"Not I. With the Society of the Far Edge, beside Le Saphir Mortel, I was content. I thought myself a king of the world. I drank absinthe and ate lotus and talked about beauty and love. And I played at cards."

Houdini sensed the narrative neared some kind of climax. "Did you win at cards?" he asked, mildly.

"At first, yes. Later my losses were considerable."

That was an old story. An innocent young man is hooked by an alluring lady into a card-school where his initial successes turn into crippling debt. "Have you a fortune back home that might alleviate these gambling dues?"

Sheffield shook his head. "Father lost most of his money when his railway stocks failed. The clubmen didn't seem to mind about my debts. I thought us friends. And then..."

"Then?" Houdini prompted. He saw tears forming in the young man's eyes that were nothing to do with the cutting winds.

"Then Diane came to find me. My sister. She was worried about me, you see, so she came to Paris to make sure I was all right."

"That was kind of her."

"She is kind. And good, and pure, and decent! Oh, what have I done?"

For a moment Houdini thought that Sheffield would throw himself to his death then and there. He almost leaped forward to try and grapple the young man. But the distressed youth got a grip of his emotions and carried on speaking.

"I wanted Diane to see that I'd prospered, that I was a regarded part of Parisian society. I introduced her to Le Saphir and to the Far Edge Club. How could I do that? How could I have been so stupid?"

Houdini felt a chill run through him. Again it was not the crosswinds.

"It was a merry evening at the Club," remembered Sheffield. "The wine flowed, the cards went my way for once. I thought Diane was my lucky charm. I had recovered nearly all my losses before the deck turned against me."

Houdini was an expert at card tricks. He knew how easily a sharp could turn a deck. "You lost what you had recovered and more," he surmised.

Sheffield nodded. "It was then, with the absinthe buzzing through my head, in that silk-lined drawing room, surrounded by Le Saphir and all those good fellows that I sealed my fate. It was then that I gambled my sister."

Houdini frowned. "What?"

"It seemed a joke at the time. Even Diane half-laughed, although she fell silent thereafter. I wagered her on a hand I could not lose."

"And lost," Houdini concluded. "Such a bet is not legal."

"Such men, such rich, powerful, ruthless men do not require the law to collect their winnings," Sheffield said. His face was bleak and without hope. "Diane is gone. Vanished. Taken, who knows where, to who knows what evil fate?" He rose to his feet again and braced himself to jump. "And so…"

"And so you'd toss yourself off the Tower and abandon her?" Houdini sneered scornfully. "Up till now I thought you were a young idiot who'd been played for a fool. Now I see you're a coward too! Your sister's kidnapped and your reaction is to kill yourself? What kind of man are you, Richard Sheffield?"

The young Englishman swallowed hard, stung to the core by the American showman's contempt. "There is nothing I can do. They will not see me. Le Saphir had me thrown out of her theatre. They deny ever having met Diane. These powerful men have unbelievable influence! I am not here as a first resort, Mr Houdini, but rather as a last one."

"So if there was another way, another chance to save Diane, would you take it?"

Sheffield nodded slowly. "Of course I would. I'd do anything."

"Then you'd better climb down with me. I'll find Diane Sheffield for you." Houdini smiled. "I usually make things disappear, but I'm betting I can make someone reappear just this once."

Sheffield tugged his bottom lip uncertainly. "They are so powerful…"

"Every trap's got a weak point," Houdini told him. "C'mon. It's not like the Eiffel Tower's going anywhere. Give helping your sister one last shot." Now he held out his hand.

Sheffield took it. "Help us, please," he begged.

"Sure thing. Let's get on this right away. Who are these powerful men that played cards with you?"

"Mostly they use *noms de voyages* at their masques," Sheffield admitted, "but their host in Paris is the Marquis de Confontaine."

"And so you'd toss yourself off the Tower and abandon her?"

Houdini recognised the name. It looked like he might be accepting M. Lascalle's invitation after all.

⁓✣⁓

M. Bertillion, Paris' Prefect de Police, had recovered from his mild chagrin about the performance of his handcuffs and his ribbing from the military officers who had supervised Houdini's confinement. An excellent *fois gras* had worked wonders on his temperament and as he climbed into the carriage waiting to take him back to his office at Place Louis Lépine[3] he was filled with sentimental warmth about Houdini and the whole day.

His mood was disrupted again when that selfsame Houdini opened his carriage door and climbed in to join him. Houdini's agent Beck followed, along with a dishevelled Englishman in his shirt-sleeves.

"Pardon our intrusion, Monsieur Bertillion," Houdini said. "I do not believe you have met Mr Sheffield?"

"Non," agreed the police officer. He made a baffled nod of acknowledgement towards the youngster. "Messieurs…"

"Mr Sheffield is missing a sister. He has not so far received much attention from the Parisian police."

Bertillion frowned. The name suddenly made connections in his mind. "Monsieur Sheffield, who played at cards with le Marquis de Confontaine? That was not a wise game, monsieur."

"I reported Diane's disappearance to the constables," Sheffield reported wearily. "They said I had no evidence of the Marquis' involvement. Many young women disappear in Paris. With no sign of foul play they had no reason to make more than routine enquiries."

"It is the case," agreed the Prefect. "I am sorry to say it to you, M. Sheffield, but girls who come to the big city sometimes lose their heads – and more delicate things. They meet a man, they fall in love, they elope…"

"Not Diane. She was only here for me, to help me. She knew no-one in Paris except the people she had met at the *Club de Bord Lointain* and amongst the circle of Le Saphir Mortel!"

Bertillion winced at the young man's denial. "Sir, these are such people as I would not want my sister to meet, and she is forty-one with grown-up children. The gentlemen of the Far Edge Club are notorious sybarites, rich

3   The Paris police force is based at Place Louis Lépine, 1 rue de Lutèce, 75004 Paris. The politically-appointed Prefect is assisted by the *prevote*, a second-in-command who is a "practical" policeman and runs the actual police-work of the department.

enough to do what they like, powerful enough to get away with it, many of them anonymous anyway. And Le Saphir is notorious, a *demi-monde* who has risen from obscurity, out of the bedrooms of Le Chabanais[4] to the stages of Montmartre."

"Perhaps these people could be questioned?" Beck suggested.

Bertillion shook his head. "It is not possible. We are a country of rules and practices, Monsieur Beck. If I send an officer to interrogate Le Saphir without good cause, tomorrow there will be a telegram on my desk from the Minister of the Interior or a Secretary of State demanding what I am about. If an officer were to disturb le Marquis..." The Prefect shuddered.

"So you intend to do nothing about this young woman?" Houdini demanded.

"I will uphold the law, of course. If you can bring me evidence, firm evidence, of some harm that has befallen her, if you can find her and she is held against her will, then I must act. But in matters of the female heart, where a *jolie fille* has loved unwisely – or perhaps lucratively – in those cases I cannot interfere."

Beck could see Houdini's temper beginning to rise. He intervened to head off trouble. "You may be able to help us in other ways then, M. Bertillion. We are newcomers to Paris. Perhaps you can tell us of this Far Edge Club and of its sponsor?"

Even that seemed a little dangerous to the Prefect. His hand trembled a little and his answer was reluctant. "There are some men for whom the thrill is everything." He glanced momentarily at Houdini. "They cannot feel alive without the threat of death – theirs or another's. When such men also possess immeasurable riches and power, well, you will understand that they acknowledge no limits. They play games without frontiers."

"What sort of games?" Houdini asked. "More than *vingt-et-un*, I'm guessing."

"Any activity wherein there lies extreme peril," Bertillion agreed.

---

4   12 rue Chabanais near the Louvre was Paris' most famous *maison de tolerance*, a legal brothel. Costing 1.7 million Francs to establish in 1878, it featured rooms in Moorish, Hindu, Pompeyan, and Louis XVI style. Its Japanese room won a design prize at the 1900 World Fair. Toulouse-Lautrec painted sixteen tableaux for the house. Guy de Maupassant built a copy of the Moorish room in his seaside home. Le Chabanais was such a favourite of Albert Edward, Prince of Wales, who became English king Edward VI in 1901, that "Dirty Bertie" kept a private room there decorated and furnished to his personal tastes, with his coat of arms above the bed. Later visitors included Cary Grant, Humphrey Bogart, Marlene Dietrich, and Herman Goering.

"Men of the Club have jumped from hot-air balloons, have rappelled over the caldera of live volcanoes, have braved river rapid falls that lesser men would never countenance. But more, they have wagered on feats of human endurance, on sports of lethal chance such as the Russian roulette, on fights to the death between man and wild beast. Or so it is said."

Sheffield moaned desolately. "Diane! What have I done?"

"If this *cadet Anglais* has lost a sister to these men he had best forget her," the Prefect advised. "He will never find her, and if he does she will be so changed that he will wish he had preserved his memory."

"Well, this American's going to find Diane Sheffield," Harry Houdini swore. "And the whole of the French cabinet can send him telegrams complaining about it after!"

⌁ ∂ℚ℮ ⌁

Le Théâtre du Grand-Guignol was the smallest public theatre in Paris, a converted chapel that still retained the confessionals as boxes. Carved angels looked over the tiny performance stage. The ecclesiastical touches gave the place a macabre atmosphere.

Houdini appreciated the showmanship. Patrons of the Guignol came for the visceral performances of works considered unfitting for the higher-brow stages. Under the theatre's founder and director Oscar Méténier it had told stories of prostitutes, criminals, street urchins, characters that would never be acknowledged in the mainstream works of conventional venues. For the past three years under the directorship of Max Maurey and his protégé playwright André de Lorde the emphasis had focussed on realistically-portrayed horror stories.

M. Cabot, the stage-manager, was eager to show the famous Harry Houdini around the rehearsal. "This is a new work but it will be our greatest triumph yet," he explained to the American. "A doctor discovers that his young wife has taken a lover. Through circumstance that lover lies helpless on the operating table beneath the doctor's knife. The doctor carves open this man's brain, cutting out parts to render him a hallucinating idiot, a mere shambling *demi-homme*, whom he looses upon his wife. The creature comes in turn against the doctor, seizing up a chisel and…[5]" Cabot smiled. "Well, M. Houdini, we judge the effectiveness of our performance by how many of our audience faint during the show. If at least two of the crowd do not pass out from shock we count our efforts a failure."

---

5   This sounds like the plot from *Le Laboratoire des Hallucinations* by André de Lorde and Henri Bauch, but that play was not staged until 1931 so perhaps this is some earlier, prototypical version.

"It must run expensive in pig's blood," Houdini noted.

On the stage the shambling horror described in the plot had corned a screaming young woman. She backed away, her low-cut nightdress barely restraining her heaving bosom. "No! It is I! Your Sonia!" she called as the monster approached her.

"Son...ia...!" the creature slurred as he pinned his victim down.

Houdini's eyebrows rose slightly as the monster tore open the actress' nightdress and simulated her violation.

"Our audiences have different tastes to yours, perhaps?" M. Cabot suggested.

"If there's blood in my performances it means something's gone wrong," Houdini admitted.

The victim's screams were silenced as a bladder of gore sprayed across the stage and onto the seats where the front row of the audience would sit.

That clearly concluded the second act rehearsal. "Bravo!" the stage-manager applauded. "A triumph. Take ten minutes to mop up and prepare for act three. Marie-Anne, come here and meet a famous American!"

The murdered woman got up. Someone handed her a towel to wipe the blood from her breasts, then passed her a robe to cover the tattered remnants of her cotton chemise.

"I enjoy meeting famous Americans," the Lethal Sapphire admitted, smiling up at Houdini. "Especially handsome ones."

"This is the illusionist Houdini," Cabot introduced. "M. Houdini, may I present our shining, incomparable star, Le Saphir Mortel?"

The actress presented her hand to be kissed. "Did you enjoy my performance, Monsieur?"[6]

"It was very memorable," Houdini replied. "However, it is not a stage matter that I have come to see you about."

The Sapphire smiled. She was used to men seeking her out for her other talents. Her silk robe dropped casually from one shoulder. "What is it you are looking for, M. Houdini?" she purred.

"Diane Sheffield," answered the escape artist.

Marie-Anne's expression changed for a moment before the actress resumed her perfect mask. "What is little Mademoiselle Sheffield to you?"

"She is a young woman who may be in great trouble. I am told you may be able to help me find her."

6   The Guignol's best-known actress was Paula Maxa. In a career spanning from 1917 to the 30s she became known as "the world's most assassinated woman", having died onstage around 10,000 times in over sixty ways, in addition to her 3,000 rapes.

"You have been listening to poor Richard, oui? I thought so. He is not well."

"I thought the same thing when I talked him off a ledge on the Eiffel Tower. He's worried sick about his sister. He said you wouldn't see him."

The Lethal Sapphire shrugged, revealing even more flesh. "It is a sad thing, when a young unworldly man finds himself beyond his… what is the word for *profondément*? Yes, as the English say, out of his depth. He comes to Paris, an innocent abroad. He learns to drink, to smoke, to dice, to love, but in his heart he is still the provincial *homme d'Anglais*, yes?"

"You knew him well, then?"

"I knew him. I blame myself in part for not realising how deep his attachment to me had grown. I do not choose to be a *blond de suicide*, to draw men to their deaths. I am the sapphire, cold and hard as I have been made. When I realised how obsessed Richard had become I turned him away."

"But not before you'd met Diane."

The actress confessed it. "He introduced me to his sister. She was like him, the *vierge innocente*. I play many such girls at the Guignol. They never end well."

On the stage the gore had been swilled and Cabot was reassembling the actors for the confrontation between the brain-maimed killer and the doctor who had lobotomised him. A bucket of entrails was being concealed under the victim's coat. The Sapphire took Houdini's arm. "I am not in this scene, except my head. That is a model, of course, the finest waxwork in Paris, imported from Madam Tussaud's of London.[7] We must retire to my dressing room. We would not wish to put the actors off their screaming."

Houdini followed the beauty offstage. Nobody seemed surprised that the Lethal Sapphire might be leading a stranger back to her chamber.

"So Diane was a virgin innocent," he interrogated Marie-Anne as they approached her door.

"Yes. Beautiful in that Saxon way, but without fire and passion – or not yet awoken. She was… *agréable*. Nice."

Houdini followed the Sapphire into her dressing room. A plump attendant helped her mistress to strip off both robe and bloodstained nightdress without shame or even a second thought.

"Richard Sheffield says you introduced the *agréable* Diane to your mutual acquaintances in the *Club de Bord Lointain*," Houdini persisted.

7　　　Anna Maria Tussaud (1761-1850) founded the famous London waxworks that still bears her name.

The Sapphire's exquisite display did not distract the American showman from his purpose.

"Yes. He wished it and she did not object. There are some fine men behind those anonymous masks, rich, handsome men who could offer a good future to a girl who caught their eye."

"And did Diane catch their eye?"

The Sapphire shrugged. "I cannot say. When I am with them I am more interested in having their eyes on me." She held her arms out so she could be washed and powdered. "I like having handsome men's eyes upon me," she pouted to Houdini.

Houdini was a man of the world. He knew how to ignore coquettes. "What of their host in Paris? Did Diane meet this Marquis de Confontaine?"

Marie-Anne's attendant stopped her preening and froze. The Lethal Sapphire's sensual pose wavered for a moment too.

"Leave us, Colette," she told the plump maid. The girl courtesyed and vanished discreetly.

The Sapphire picked up her robe and pulled it on. This time she wrapped it tight and closed it to her neck. She lifted a cigarette from a silver box and lit it on the third attempt.

"The Marquis?" Houdini prompted.

"I do not like to talk about le Marquis," Marie-Anne replied. "Can we not discuss more pleasant things, Monsieur? Or come to my couch and we will not speak at all."

"De Confontaine scares you? Why?"

The Sapphire swallowed hard. "Please? I am a beautiful woman. Take pleasure in me, M. Houdini, and ask no more."

"He does not scare me, Mademoiselle le Saphir. Tell me about him. Please."

The Sapphire's cigarette trembled as she put it to her lips. "Le Marquis de Confontaine," she confided, "He is the Devil."

Screams came from the stage above as the *zombi* went to work with his chisel.

"He is the Devil," the Sapphire repeated. "When other men might die he simply laughs. Bullets cannot harm him. I have seen him place a revolver to his head, pull the trigger, take the bullet… then laugh and hand the gun to the man opposite him and demand that his opponent takes his turn!"

"That's possible with a clever use of blanks and trickery," Houdini objected.

"And knives, m'sieu? And epée? Fire does not burn him, and why should it? No mortal flame can match the inferno below."

"There are chemicals that insulate the skin from flame for a time. Fire-eaters use them. I know the trick myself."

The Sapphire shook her head. "He is not a conjurer. He is a vessel for some Abyssal power, some diabolic intelligence that rides him like a chariot. What looks out from the windows of his eyes, it is not human, nor ever was." She turned away. "His tastes are… unpleasant. I am no stranger to debauchery, M. Houdini. A girl must make her way in this world. I have seen many disgusting, degrading acts and done most of them. But I would rather whore for *sous* in the gutters of Pigalle than surrender myself to a night with le Marquis. De Sade himself would be sickened by de Confontaine's amusements."

Houdini's lips tightened. "And you introduced Diane Sheffield to this man?"

Marie-Anne would not meet his eyes. "When one is escaping a tiger that is faster and stronger than anything one could imagine, one does not seek to outdistance it. One can only hope that some other prey occupies its attention. Something softer and more tender for it to devour while you get away."

"Did you throw Miss Sheffield to the Marquis, then, to save your skin?"

"Do not look at me like that, Monsieur. You have not seen those eyes. You have not experienced… It was Richard who played the cards, not I. It was he who accepted the stakes, while the roués of the *Bord Lointain* looked on and laughed. Do not judge me!"

"Does the Marquis hold Diane now?" Houdini demanded.

The Lethal Sapphire collapsed. She fell to the floor and began to sob like a child. "I do not know! How can I? I do not wish her ill! I do not seek her death! But the gentlemen of the Far Edge Club are above the law. A word from them and one night my rape and death on that stage will not be imaginary. And the Marquis will catch my soul and drag me down to hell!"

"This Marquis de Confontaine," Houdini questioned. "Where do I find him?"

"I have seen portraits of his father and grand-father and his ancestors before that," the Sapphire whispered. "They all look the same. Each of them, every generation, exactly like the Marquis. It is the same man, immortal, evil, unstoppable!"

"Where is he?"

"He will destroy you, American. He will kill you and damn you!"

"I'll take my chances. Where do I look?"

The Sapphire cradled her head in her hands. Her glorious blonde hair spilled over her face and shoulders as she wept. "He has a house in St Germain on rue de Verneuil," she confessed at last. "Do not go there, Houdini. You will never come out alive!"

~ひⱤ℗~

The room was papered in red Chinese silk. The tall classical windows were draped with velvet. The cut glass chandeliers were plated with gold. The card table was Louis XIV.

The men and women who watched as Houdini picked up his card wore evening dress, the men impeccably tailored in black suits and stiff brocaded shirts with white ties or sleek cravats, the women in long shimmering gowns cut low and daring. All of them worse black half-face masks to disguise themselves, or to give the illusion of disguise.

Houdini picked up the card. It was the five of spades.

He kept his hand close. Any of the three dozen spectators might be working with the dealer, looking over the players' shoulders and making seemingly-innocent gestures to signal what each deal gave. He added the five to his existing collection: a three, a six, and a two.

He had sixteen points in his hand. In *vingt-et-un* the objective was to draw cards of values up to but not beyond twenty-one. More points than that and the hand was "bust", the wager forfeit. If the dealer drew equal or lower than the hand that Houdini settled on – "stuck" on – then the wager was likewise lost. Only by gaining points as close to 21 as possible could the player prevail.[8]

The crowd watched excitedly. The game had gone on for half an hour now. Almost the whole deck had been dealt at some point; only four cards remained on the pile the dealer had shuffled and Houdini had cut. The bet on the table amounted to some twelve thousand francs.[9]

The other players had all dropped out. Only Houdini and the inscrutable dealer remained in the game.

The onlookers murmured and whispered. They could not know what the showman held, but they knew that the upturned card of the two before the dealer was the Queen of Diamonds – ten points. Another picture card, with a full-deck likelihood of 3/13, would give the dealer a score of twenty,

---

8   Card players will recognise the similarities to the modern games of Blackjack or Pontoon, of which this turn-of-19th-century version was a forerunner.

9   This was about $2,500 dollars at a time when the average annual household income in the US was $438. In modern money there was around $250,000 on the table.

requiring the full twenty-one to beat. An ace would count as eleven and would make a "pontoon", a score that could only be beaten by a five-card trick. Five cards amounting to anything under twenty-two was unbeatable even by the ace-picture card combination. So the question in their minds was would Houdini attempt to draw another card to go for five?

While the crowd's minds raced to the odds, Houdini was making a different and more informed calculation. His trained brain had memorised the cards dealt and played. He knew that the four remaining cards in the dealer's deck and the hidden card by the dealer's hand must be the nine of diamonds, the ace of clubs, the two and four of spades, and the eight of hearts. Three out of five of them would provide him with a five card trick; two would bust him.

Even the five card trick would not guarantee him success. Once he had rested his hand, the dealer too would draw to attempt the highest possible score without busting. Those same low cards might assist him in assembling a second five-card trick that would trump Houdini's hand.

The odds favoured Houdini, but not overwhelmingly. "*Tortillon*," the showman said, indicating his desire for another card.

The dealer passed him the top card on the downward-facing deck. Houdini peered at its corner. It was the six of spades - and the six of spades had already been played. It should have been in the discard pile.

The crowd was watching. Across the room the Marquis de Confontaine stood with Martin Beck, M. Lascalle, and Le Saphir Mortel, staring intently at the American player who had appeared uninvited at his St Germain mansion and crashed the party.

The dealer had cheated, presumably with his host's permission. Houdini's conscience was clear.

"*Cinq tour de cartes*," Houdini announced. He laid his five card trick on the antique baize: three of hearts, two and six of clubs, five of spades – and the five of diamonds!

Houdini had toured doing card tricks long before he ever demonstrated his first escape.

The dealer's brows rose. Houdini smiled at him. The audience clapped and shouted "Bravo!"

Martin Beck breathed again. Houdini had come very close to bankrupting them both.

"He is a player, your Houdini," the Marquis said to the manager.

"Yes, sir, he is," Beck agreed. "I hope you don't mind that he decided to take up Monsieur Lascalle's invitation at the last minute?"

"Au contraire. I am very gratified that he has chosen to enter my home," de Confontaine replied. He moved forward, clapping politely. "Your reputation does not disappoint, M. Houdini. I begin to believe that you are as talented as your namesake inspiration."

Houdini nodded in acknowledgement of the compliment. "Every magician on every stage of the world owes a debt to Robert-Houdin, the father of our art. I am pleased at last to come to his city and follow in his footsteps."[10]

"And we are pleased to receive you at the Far Edge Club. Can we hope that you are now willing to consider our challenge to your skills? Or would you prefer to play at cards a little more?"

Houdini took his hands from the card table. "I think I've had enough wagering for one night. I'll give it up while I'm ahead." He met the Marquis' stare. "I hear that some of your guests bet more than they can afford to lose."

De Confontaine smiled thinly. His lips curved but his eyes remained cold. "Unless the wager is more than one can afford there is no *frisson.* Life without *frisson* is death."

"Is that what you told Richard Schofield when he lost his sister?"

Beck looked around the room uneasily. In addition to the masked guests there were a number of burly footmen whose renaissance wigs and livery did nothing to disguise their bulk. The Lethal Sapphire remained motionless, her face as much of a mask as the black silk creation that obscured it.

The Marquis reached the card table. The dealer hastily vacated his seat so his master could sit. "You are interested in the lady? The mademoiselle Diane Sheffield is a *belle femme fraîche* that would please any man's eye."

"I'm interested in where she is and what's happened to her," Houdini replied.

The Marquis shuffled the deck in his long pale hands. "Interested enough to dare one more wager, perhaps?" He dealt the top four cards, peeling four aces onto the table. "What game shall we play?"

Houdini was prepared. "You mentioned a challenge. What was it?"

The Marquis gestured for Lascalle to come forward and speak. "Beneath Paris there are tunnels," the lawyer said. "Many were mine shafts, dating to medieval and even Roman times. Later they were occupied during the

---

10   Houdini took his stage name from the "father of conjuring", Jean Eugène Robert-Houdin (1805-1871), who pioneered modern stage magic. Houdini replicated many of Robert-Houdin's tricks, adding additional twists to make them even more impossible.

Terror, then used as boneyards when the great cemeteries overflowed. Six million Parisians lie in charnel houses beneath our feet."

"Lovely," breathed Beck.

"These old tunnels were overlaid with Napoleon's sewers, with passageways opened between houses during the time of the Commune, with many private passageways. No city in the world has deeper or more complex underground workings than Paris. It is there, in that labyrinth, that we have set our challenge."

"You are accustomed to escaping, Houdini," the Marquis declared. "We shall lock you in a sealed chamber beyond the burial catacombs, inside that maze of waterways and secret passages. If you can escape to the surface before dawn then you will win. If not – you lose."

"Wait a moment," Beck objected. "What are the stakes?"

"If M. Houdini succeeds, he will find the lady he seeks. She will be unharmed, free to go. If he fails, then he loses... his reputation. The lady loses... more." The Marquis raised one eyebrow at the showman. "Well?"

"When?" Houdini asked.

"Tomorrow night," de Confontaine suggested. "The Far Edge Club had a different celebration planned, but your efforts will be more entertaining yet. And should you fail then our other amusement will still remain available to us."

"I've heard it said that you are the Devil," Houdini told the Marquis. "The Devil keeps his word when he's made a pact."

"In that we are the same," de Confontaine assured him. "You will have a chance. Where is the sport otherwise? And you will feel the thrill of living – at the far edge."

Houdini held out his hand. "Then I accept the challenge," he said. "It's a bet."

⁓ɔ𝕏ᶜ⁓

"This is madness!" Beck objected the next day. He paced the empty stage of the theatre he'd been considering hiring for his client's Paris debut. His footsteps echoed in the deserted auditorium and kicked up ghosts of dust. "Houdini, there are rumoured to be over a hundred miles of tunnels beneath this city. In addition to the great ossuaries there are aqueducts and mines, limestone caverns, eroded bell-holes, pits, dead-falls... the whole place is a death trap."

"Exactly that, I suspect," Houdini admitted. "But it is a trap I must enter and escape if I am to find Diane alive."

"Then I accept the challenge. It's a bet."

"You have to help her," Richard Sheffield pleaded. The young Englishman still trailed after his only hope for his sister's salvation. "She is innocent. It is I that should pay for being so foolish, not she."

"We won't abandon her," Houdini promised. "I've taken a mighty big dislike to that Marquis de Confontaine. If he is the Devil then I want to tweak his nose – preferably like St Dunstan did, with red-hot tongs!"[11]

"Do not underestimate the Marquis," Sheffield warned. "He is a deadly enemy, cunning and cruel."

"Every trap has a flaw," the escape artist replied. He bowed formally as if to a crowd, kicked his heels, and vanished through a stage-trap that Beck and Sheffield hadn't even known was there. Houdini's voice came from the props room below. "The trick is finding it."

～♋～

The Marquis' Left Bank mansion was full of candles. They cast a yellow glow over the elegant creatures that assembled for the entertainment. The men were all powerful, the women all beautiful. Their velvet masks concealed their faces and their secrets.

The gaunt Lascalle led Houdini from the room where the escapologist had been thoroughly searched. Now Houdini wore different evening dress, perfectly tailored to his measurements but lacking the lockpicks, knife blades, hooks and other instruments cunningly concealed in his original ensemble. Lascalle had even required him to regurgitate the pouch of thieves' tools he had swallowed.

The showman was the only unmasked person in the long drawing room. He processed past the members of the Far Edge Club and their chattels, speculating on their identities. He had no difficulty in recognising the intense stare of the Marquis de Confontaine.

The magician's aristocratic host wore a peacock-blue jacket embroidered with elaborate gold appliqué. He carried a serpent-headed swagger cane in his fingertips. He was not accompanied tonight by Le Saphir but was flanked by two Nubian beauties who never spoke and never took their hands from his shoulders.

---

11   A popular folk-legend held that 8th century Anglo-Saxon monk St Dunstan identified a woman tempting him as actually being the Devil by spotting her hidden tail. He used the red-hot tongs heused the red-hot tongs with which he was forging a communion chalice to seize Satan's nose: "St. Dunstan, as the story goes/ Once pulled the Devil by the nose/ With red-hot tongs, which made him roar/ That he was heard three miles or more."

Houdini did not approach the Marquis, although that was clearly what the aristocrat expected. Instead the escape artist sat at the same chair where he had played cards the night before and waited for de Confontaine to join him at the table.

The Marquis took the seat opposite. "He has signed the papers?" he asked Lascalle.

"Oui. If an accident befalls M. Houdini we are indemnified from blame. All risks are his."

Houdini stated straight ahead, his hands on his lap, ignoring the exchange.

"The terms, then," the Marquis said to him directly. "You wager your reputation that you can escape the prison maze that is prepared for you in the catacombs below, before dawn breaks six hours from now. I wager the fair Diane Sheffield."

"You also undertake that there is actually a feasible way out," Houdini prompted.

"It is so. But you will understand that I do not say it is easy."

Houdini nodded.

"There is a tunnel beneath this house that leads to a part of the Parisian underworld that we have specially prepared for our revels," the Marquis announced. "We will take you there, shackle you, and leave you. You may seek escape and you may find the lady."

Houdini looked up sharply. "Diane?"

De Confontaine looked pleased at the showman's unease. "Indeed. She remains unharmed and unspoiled, as I promised. But she is also in considerable peril tonight, not from me but from where she happens to be. If you escape your bonds and your prison you may, of course, immediately make for the surface. But the *belle fille* may come to harm, not through any agency of mine but merely by neglect."

"So I don't just have to get out, I've got to find and rescue Miss Sheffield too!"

"You do not have to," the Marquis noted. "Think of it as a choice."

"Anything else?"

"One small thing. We of the Far Edge Club enjoy extremes. We find pleasure in danger, ours or another's. We enjoy all kinds of adventurous sports – especially hunting. Tonight was shall be indulging our passion for seeking prey in the tunnels of Paris, the very same charnel passages that you may be using for your exit. Be most careful, M. Houdini, that none of us mistakes you for legitimate quarry."

"You and your buddies will be down there with rifles looking for me," Houdini translated. "The kid gloves are off."

The Marquis examined the delicate white gloves on his thin hands. "Goatskin is so crude," he observed. "Human flesh is much softer."

"Let's get on with this," Houdini growled.

"Your idol, Robert-Houdin, was said to be able to catch a bullet in his teeth," de Confontaine remembered. "I wonder if you can do the same trick, without the preparation and slight-of-hand?"

Houdini didn't reply.

～◌◌◌◌～

Two hundred and sixty-one irregular steps down; the blindfolded escapologist was walked along a cobbled corridor, through a creaking gate, along a shallow path beside running water. Seventy-three paces from the gate he was spun around three and a quarter turns then led south down a tunnel shallow enough to require him to bend.

It was ten minutes before Houdini's captors halted him, although he calculated that he had been walked in a circle for part of it. His hood was removed so he could see the bell-shaped underground chamber where they'd brought him. A circular steel lid covered part of the floor.

With Houdini were four of the Marquis' burly footmen, a dozen favoured members of the Far Edge Club, and Etienne-Louis de Confontaine himself. The Marquis' eyes seemed to spark redly in the light of his flunkies' oil lanterns.

A wooden chest yielded heavy manacles. Half-inch chains locked around Houdini's ankles and wrists. More joined his elbows together behind his back. A metal collar attached a heavy metal ball on a six-foot shackle.

"Is that it?" Houdini challenged.

"Not quite," the Marquis replied. "Hold him!"

Houdini could hardly struggle as the brutal footmen immobilised him further. Confontaine took a leather case from his dinner jacket pocket and opened it to reveal a hypodermic syringe.

"Hold on…" Houdini objected.

"Poison, of course," the Marquis admitted, "but slow acting. You will not begin to feel its effects before morning. After that debilitation will come quickly, but death will be slow and agonising." He stabbed the needle into Houdini's arm.

"Murder, then!" snarled the showman.

The Marquis held up a glass ampoule. "This is the antidote. It is very effective. All you need do is retrieve it from me. Of course, that may change your escape route plans again."

"Oh, I was coming to look for you anyway," Houdini promised.

"I fear this will be out last meeting, American," de Confontaine answered. "I'd bet your life on it."

His servants drew back steel bolts on the floor-grate. They hinged the lid open to reveal a lower chamber, dark and full of churning water right up to the brim.

"You might want to take a deep breath now," the Marquis mocked Houdini. "Ready?"

The magician hyperventilated, flooding his body with oxygen. The Marquis' thug punched him in the belly to force him to exhale again.

Houdini was tossed through the hole. The heavy chains on his limbs and neck dragged him down into the lightless torrent.

The lid was replaced to leave him sinking in the airless darkness.

⸚ℬ⸱

The Place de la Condorde lit up at night, shining through the wet gloom like an expressionist painting. Houdini's suite in the Hôtel de Crillon offered spectacular views of Paris by night, but Martin Beck had no time for them. He paced up and down muttering angrily to himself.

"I should never have let Houdini do this foolishness. He shouldn't have gone alone. He shouldn't have insisted. I should call the police. I should call the press. I should have done something to stop him."

Richard Sheffield downed another glass of wine with trembling hands. "I'm sorry," he groaned. "I'm so sorry."

Beck realised that the young Englishman must be even tenser than he. "You were a fool, but you know that," he told Sheffield. "But this isn't a situation of your making."

The boy turned away.

Something about his reaction sparked a flicker of suspicion in Houdini's manager. "Is there something you're not saying?"

"No. Of course not." Sheffield tried to lift his glass again but he shook too badly.

Beck stood over him. "Listen, my client and my friend's risking his life right now for your sister, so if there's something I should know you'd better damn well spit it out!"

Sheffield cradled his head in his hands. "I am the most wretched creature!"

"I don't really care. What does bother me is that Houdini's out there without back-up and you seem to know more than you're spilling. So talk!"

When Sheffield looked up there were tears in his eyes. "They had Diane. You must understand – they had my sister. Those men. Those monsters. The things they planned for her! These cruel men in this cruel city, all their venom and lust focussed on poor sweet Diane! I had no choice."

Beck's eyebrows furrowed. "You weren't out on the Tower by coincidence that day?" he guessed. "It was a set up? That shyster Lascalle, probably, when I turned down his offer."

"They told me if I didn't deliver Mr Houdini to them, didn't get him to play their game, they would… well, it doesn't matter what they threatened. I did it. I sacrificed your friend, a good man, to keep my sister whole."

"So what's this Marquis got planned for Houdini?"

"I don't know."

Beck took Sheffield by the lapels. "So tell me what you do know."

The young man confessed.

Beck went to get his revolver – and his wallet!

⚬⚭⚬

The ball and chain on Houdini's neck sank him to the bottom of the water channel. It was a blessing in some ways because it prevented him from being snatched by the current and dragged through one of the enclosed vents that drained the tank.

Houdini estimated that he had three minutes to find air. He'd steeled his stomach for the blow; taking punches above the belt from any man was a regular part of his repertoire and he'd hardly lost any of the oxygen in his lungs. Now he had to ditch his chains.

Houdini unfolded the tiny pouch of tools in his hand. He'd been thoroughly searched before, but then they'd brought him to the same table he'd occupied to play cards. Why else would he have visited the Marquis before tonight if not to plant a roll of housebreaking implements under the Louis XIV table?

Working by touch in the absolute blackness of the underwater tank, Houdini found the right lockpick to spring the cuffs at his wrists. They were easy. He brought his manacled feet up and unlocked them too. He'd spent thirty seconds.

The elbow-cuffs were more difficult. They restricted him from bringing his arms in front of him and were beyond his hands' reach to pick. The underwater setting precluded using his tiny capsule of sulphuric acid to dissolve the chain. There was no time or angle to rely upon his miniature keyhole saw.

Houdini concentrated, gritted his teeth, and popped his left shoulder out of its socket. As the muscles screamed he wrenched his right arm up, slithering it out of the metal gyve, twisting until it was free. He had to hold back a gasp of pain that would have cost him precious air. At two minutes, one arm was loose. He forced the other limb back into place, clenching his teeth.

The neck manacle was of a different design, delicate and tiny. Houdini's fingers were numbing in the freezing water; he almost dropped the tiny pin he required to turn the micro-tumblers.

At two minutes thirty-two seconds the collar opened, freeing him from the heavy ball that pinioned him to the tank's base. The current tried to drag him to the vents but Houdini fought it. His estimate of the Marquis' psychology was that there would be additional traps that way; a grill perhaps, or some impassable blockage or deadfall. Instead he struck out with all his strength against the press of the water, seeking its ingress.

His senses began to blur. Purple spots appeared before his eyes despite the lightless silo. He found the tunnel that the water surged in through and pressed up it by main strength.

At three minutes fifteen seconds his numbed hands found a gap in the ceiling. Houdini hauled himself through the old fracture where the roof had collapsed, and found precious air.

Although he climbed no more than twenty feet it took him quarter of an hour to slither through the tight crack, scraping his bulk against the jagged edges of the natural cleft. He broke out into a dry chamber above and lay there gasping and exhausted.

But not for long. Nearby voices alerted him to new danger. Houdini rolled aside and found cover behind a pile of rotted casks. A light appeared off in a side passage. He only glimpsed shadows of two men carrying rifles who passed by chatting pleasantly as if out shooting partridges.

In darkness once again, Houdini took stock of his situation. The Far Edge Club was hunting him. He would not put it past the Marquis to send divers into the water system to seek his downed body. When it was not found the search would intensify. He had to keep moving.

He secured a barrel spar as a makeshift weapon and moved by touch to the tunnel he'd seen. He chose the opposite direction to the one the hunters had taken. If their search was leading them deeper, he reasoned, then the way they had come made more sense.

His fingers went to his life-preserving toolkit again. He found the oil-wrapped pocketbook of matches and flared one of them to life.

The tunnel was crumbling and irregular, one of the seventeenth century stone-quarry shafts. Occasional antique graffiti varied between the crude and the sacred. Houdini's tiny compass showed the mine running north-north-west, towards the Seine.

The corridor was intersected by other passageways and crossed two larger chambers. One of these offered Houdini what he required, a larger space that still retained the rotting furnishings of a mine office, cabinets and a desk filled with mouldy papers. Even damp as they were, the documents burned well from a single match-flame.

Thick smoke fumed up from the desk drawer. The wind currents pushed it along one of the passageways, indicating a possible exit. Houdini did not immediately follow, however. He cloaked himself in the darkness beyond the fire and waited.

"This way!" someone called in French. The smoke had been detected.

"Careful," a second speaker warned. "It might be him."

Two velvet-masked revellers entered the chamber hefting expensive hunting rifles. Houdini let them get close to the burning desk so their night-vision was compromised before taking the nearer man down with a scientifically-delivered throat-punch. As the other swung round, Houdini caught his rifle barrel and twisted it away.

"Let's do this up close," the showman suggested as he slammed the hunter into the wall and clamped a hand on the man's neck.

The man struggled until a gut-blow took the fight out of him.

Houdini tore the clubman's mask away. A wide-eyed rabbity face stared back at him, horrified that the hunter and hunted were reversed.

"Feeling alive at the brink of death?" Houdini asked him.

"Don't... don't hurt me," the aristocrat pleaded.

Houdini sneered at the coward. "Diane Sheffield. Where is she?"

His captive swallowed hard. "The... the pump room. That way."

"And de Confontaine?"

"I don't know. He can be anywhere. Don't make me talk about him."

"What's the way out?"

"There's a spiral stair beyond the ossuary or some ladders into private houses. All guarded. We came down the passage from the Marquis' mansion. It's past the pump room, over the stone bridge."

"How many hunters?"

"Twenty-two, and their bagmen." The clubman twitched. "What are you going to do to me?"

Houdini showed him, delivering a roundhouse right that smashed the hunter to the floor.

He searched the fallen men and confiscated rifles, ammunition, a hunting knife, two lighters, a cigar case, two fat wallets, a pocketwatch, a snuff box, two pairs of diamond cufflinks, and a monocle. Every little helped. He dragged the downed hunters into the old cupboards and blocked them in with broken chairs.

He glanced at the borrowed watch. It was now one twenty-eight a.m. Dawn came at five-seventeen. Who knew when the Marquis' poison would cut in?

Houdini slipped away to find the pump room and Miss Diane Sheffield.

*

Even past two in the morning there were still plenty of low drinking holes still open in Montmartre. Beck found one of the seediest in the alleys beside the Moulin Rouge and stepped inside.

"Is there any man here who wants to earn ten francs cash for doing a little violence?" he shouted.

The room quietened. He had their attention.

"Anybody who doesn't mind busting heads tonight come with me," Beck said.

*

The tunnels of Paris intersected the Napoleonic sewers and storm drains. One such confluence was directly beneath St Germain de Pres. On the surface Rue de Rennes and Rue Bonaparte crossed Boulevard St Germain. Far below, forgotten channels directed floodwaters to the modern pumphouse at Quai Malacais.

The older underground chamber was arched and vaulted. A stone parapet lined two walls. A further wooden walkway intersected the room, mere feet above the algae-covered reservoir. Rusting winding gear still depended from the ceiling, legacy of a time when floodgates had operated below the waterline and an artesian screw had drawn the rank waters to a higher runoff.

It was from these old chains that Diane Sheffield hung, her tied feet dangling mere inches from the reservoir's surface. Torches had been left so she could see the long shapes shifting in the waters below.

It was rumoured that crocodiles bred in the Paris waterways. The Marquis had taken no chances and had imported his own.

The only new mechanism was the clockwork device that ticked away high out for reach near the shadow-flecked roof. Every quarter hour it chimed and released another turn of the chain from which Diane hung. Every fifteen minutes brought her nearer to the hungry reptiles' jaws.

Nor was Diane Sheffield alone with the starving crocodiles. Mirroring her plight on the other side of the bridge dangled the Lethal Sapphire.

Neither woman was happy about it.

Houdini picked the lock on the rusty metal door to the pump room with some difficulty. It wasn't a complex mechanism, but was too huge for his delicate tools to turn. He improvised by drawing a nail from a discarded packing crate.

The iron portal screeched open. Houdini winced at the sound and wished he'd had space to include a can of oil in his equipment roll. He slipped through the narrow gap he'd made and found the ledge across from the gears where Diane and Marie-Anne hung.

"Houdini!" the Lethal Sapphire called out. "*Aidez-moi!*"

"That's him?" Diane Sheffield asked. Le Saphir Mortel had explained how they had become bait to trap the American escape artist. She'd expected the hero to be taller.

The clockwork chimed and dropped the women another six inches towards the water. Their trailing feet almost touched its scummy surface now. Grey logs began to move, suddenly interested.

"Free me!" Marie-Anne pleaded. "There are two wheels on the column there. Turn the one on the left. It will wind me in, away from these monsters!"

"It's not that simple, Mr Houdini!" Diane called. "Whichever wheel you choose, the other chain will be instantly released. One of us must plunge into these waters – to our death!"

Houdini detected another of the Marquis' cruel amendments to the challenge.

The crocodiles formed v-shaped waves as they moved to investigate the women. Diane and the Sapphire hung by their wrists and tried to bring their knees high for as long as their strength held out.

"M. Houdini, I am Le Saphir Mortel," called Marie-Anne. "Men pay five hundred francs, offer up their ancestral jewels, for one night in my bed. Save me. I can give you so much more than any pale English virgin!"

Diane had other concerns. "My brother, is he all right? Is Richard alive?"

Houdini examined the mechanism that held the captives over the water. The gears were sealed inside a welded box to prevent tampering. The huge wheels turned larger cogs up at the roof beyond the illusionist's reach. "I'm going to get you both out," Houdini promised, "Somehow."

"The Marquis said that this was a trap you would pin yourself in," Diane reported.

Houdini tested the chains. He couldn't haul them in. A ratchet somewhere prevented them being coiled back.

"I'm here to rescue you, Miss Sheffield," he tried to reassure the English girl. "You too, Sapphire, even though I'm surprised to find you in this situation. Did the Marquis punish you for directing me to him?"

Le Saphir Mortel's laugh was low and bitter. "Non, monsieur. He did this because it entertained him. He needs no other reason."

A crocodile broke the water's surface directly below Diane. She screamed as it snapped upwards hopefully.

Houdini forced himself to concentrate. Counterweights ensured that if one woman was released the other would plunge to her death. If one were reeled in the other would fall. Unless both women were freed at the same time then one would die.

The quarter hour was approaching. The Sapphire's promises became more urgent and graphic. Diane bit back tears as she forced herself to hang with knees to her chest while hungry reptiles waited below and snapped at the hem of her nightgown.

Houdini emptied the powder from a box of ammunition into the hunter's snuff box and improvised an impromptu explosive capsule. That and six rounds fired into the water nearby scared the crocodiles away – for now.

"If you are indeed to save us, sir, it must be soon," Diane warned.

Houdini agreed. He tested the chains again that ran from the wheel mechanism up to the larger cogs above. No amount of force would pull them back. That meant they would bear his weight. He shinned up the twin columns of links until he was twenty feet above the stone walkway, where the chains passed through metal collars to hold them straight before fitting into the grooved wheels beside the ancient gears.

He pulled the diamond cufflinks from his pocket and packed them round the left-hand chain aperture. The diamonds were the only things he had that would not be crushed by the massive weights of the machinery.

Time was almost up. Houdini shimmied down and grasped the right hand wheel to save Diane.

"*Non!*" shrieked Le Saphir Mortel, terrified at what would come next.

Houdini pulled the heavy wheel round, cranking the English girl back from the crocodiles.

The wheel-box released its hold on the Sapphire's chain to plunge her to

"I'm going to get you both out—Somehow."

her doom; except that the links crunched onto the diamonds and jammed at the guide collar. Marie-Anne fell no more than an inch, although she screamed as if she were already being devoured. Her time rehearsing at the Guignol had not been wasted.

Houdini wound in Diane's chain until she swung within reach. He hooked her close so he could pick the manacles at her wrist. She clung to him desperately as he heaved her onto the platform. "Thank you. Thank you," she breathed.

Still holding the chain that she had dangled from, Houdini turned the left wheel. It no longer connected to the Sapphire's chain but it loosed Diane's. Houdini pulled the whole length free and used it to improvise a rope to hook the dangling courtesan to where he could free her too.

The clock chimed, but the crocodiles went hungry.

"We have to get out of here," Diane advised. "The Marquis will be back!"

Houdini glanced at his watch. It was a quarter to three.

The chiming triggered another mechanism inside the cunning machine. The iron door ground shut and refastened with a metallic thunk of deadbolts. At the same time water began to gush from two channels, raising the pump room's water levels.

"Another trap," Houdini snarled. He imagined de Confontaine laughing as he'd planned this. Rescuing the women had triggered another means of death.

"Shoot the reptiles!" the Sapphire demanded. She picked up one of the captured rifles and fired blindly into the churning waters.

"That won't work," the escape artist said, seizing the gun and emptying it. "We can't even see them in this bubbling mess. We don't know how many there are or where they'll come from."

"In a few moments these rising waters will top over this path," Diane observed.

Houdini agreed. Already his creative mind had devised an escape. "We'll need to get out the same way the water's coming in, through one of those vents. I'll rig these two chains to let me swing across with each of you. If we get it right we can avoid the crocs."

"And if we don't?" questioned the Lethal Sapphire.

"Then you finally pay for all the men whose lives you've ruined," Diane told her.

The first of the torches fizzled out as the waters topped it. The foaming liquid washed over the walkway, covering the fugitives' ankles, soaking the hems of Diane and the Sapphire's sheer white nightgowns.

Houdini noted that the clockwork mechanism was still beating. He decided it would be best to depart before any other surprises were unleashed at the next quarter-hour. He hauled the chains into place where he could use one as a secure cross-line so the other could be used for a pendulum-swing.

"Who wants to try first?" he asked the women.

Diane volunteered. She wrapped herself round the adventurer and clung to him. He climbed the sealed mechanism box for height, pulled back as far as he could, then launched himself on the chain-rope. They brushed the foaming surface of the rising water and crashed into the far wall. Houdini nearly lost his grip on the chain but his other hand caught the lip of the vent. Water poured down on him and Diane, trying to drag them into the turmoil below.

"Hold the chain," he spluttered to the Englishwoman. He needed both hands to resist the drag of the gushing torrent.

The arm he'd dislocated earlier almost failed him, but with his last strength he managed to drag himself and Diane into the mouth of the water channel. Diane was able to wedge herself with her back to the top of the pipe so she would not be washed back into the pump room.

"Don't leave me!" shrieked the Lethal Sapphire, at the edge of terror.

Houdini retrieved the pendulum-chain and swung back to her. She retreated screaming as one of the crocodiles came from the depths and snapped at him.

Houdini twisted away just in time. Those killer jaws did no more than tear the leg of his pants. He responded with a pocketful of snuff into the reptile's eyes and a quick stab of hunting knife. The crocodile tore away, taking the blade with it, and retreated into the churning water.

"We shall die here!" Marie-Anne sobbed. "Yet this is not the cruellest death le Marquis could have given me!"

Houdini forced her to hold tight to him and climbed for another swing. The waters were noticeably higher in just ten minutes. This time the lowest point of the arc trailed them right into the water, slowing their passage.

Houdini's fingers scrabbled for the edge of the water-vent. He hadn't enough reach. His nails scraped the edge but the pressure of the incoming flood pushed him away.

Diane caught his wrist and held on. "Hurry!" she cried. "I can't do this for long!"

Houdini abandoned the chain. It swung away and was lost. He committed himself to closing his fingers on the lip of the inlet. He held on by his tips. The Sapphire screamed, then choked as the gushing water soaked her. The showman hauled them up into the opening.

"We're alive!" Diane gasped as Houdini and Marie-Anne joined her in the narrow tunnel.

The mechanism chimed again. The force of the water in the channel doubled.

Houdini braced himself against the edges of the pipe. Diane was slammed into him, almost dislodging him. Behind him the Lethal Sapphire grabbed his neck in a chokehold, desperate not to be washed away.

The torrent now filled the pipe. There was no air to breathe, no way to escape. Movement against the water's pressure was impossible. If Houdini relaxed his tension on the inlet's walls for a moment they would all be swept away, back into the flooded pump room with its starving Nile reptiles. Even if the Sapphire's hands on his throat had allowed breath there was nothing for him to fill his lungs with but icy Seine backwash.

Somewhere in those nightmare moments the grip on Houdini's neck vanished. The Lethal Sapphire was gone.

As Houdini reached the end of his capacity the waters diminished again. Whatever great tank had been discharged by the Marquis' mechanism was exhausted now. Houdini slumped with Diane in the waist-high current that still rushed along the pipe.

Diane was not breathing.

Houdini pushed her soaking frame up against one slime-crusted wall and forced the water from her lungs, then reinflated them with the kiss of life. Time lost meaning as he worked to save Diane Sheffield's life.

She gasped at last, and her lips moved under his. She choked up fluid and coughed. She lived!

Houdini ensured she was well braced against the wash then crawled back to the outlet where the pipe disgorged into the pump room. A single torch still flared above the rising torrent.

The crocodiles tore at the bloody flesh of the Lethal Sapphire. Her death had been as gory as any she had acted at the Grand Guignol.

Houdini spat an oath and planned his reunion with the Marquis de Confontaine.

⚶

The official entrance to the Paris catacombs is the western pavilion of Paris's former Barrière d'Enfer city gate. A narrow spiral stairwell descends nineteen meters into curving tangled halls of mortared stone. A model of Port-Mahon fortress, scuplted by a former Quarry Inspector, marks the way to the ossuary.

The lackeys who guarded the route to prevent Houdini's escape had switched from their formal livery and powdered wigs to more practical dark jackets and heavy boots. They waited silently with heavy cudgels and vicious billhooks to deter the showman from trying to leave the party early.

They were alert for a man seeking exit from the twisting bone-lined chasm. They had not expected a drunken rabble from above. Martin Beck unleashed his drinking-house mob onto the Marquis' thugs and stood well back.

At first the two sides seemed evenly matched, but Beck had emptied one of the rowdiest bars of Montmatre at just the time when the rough drinkers were ready for a fight. The burly retainers of the Far Edge Club were outnumbered by men as brutal as they.

Beck stood back as the Montmartre mob delivered a beating. Then he wisely passed his entire wallet's contents to the largest of the thugs and left the distribution of rewards to him.

As soon as the way was clear Beck moved along the narrow passage down to the ossuary gate. The carving over the entrance translated as 'Stop. This is the Empire of Death.'

"Houdini?" Beck called. "Are you hiding nearby?"

He was not surprised when the magician melted out of the shadows.

"What are you up to, Beck? How did you know I'd be here?"

"I've seen you before, Houdini. And I have to protect my investment. I found out the Marquis cheated so I decided to even the odds. Can we go now?"

There were still the problems of getting Diane Sheffield from where Houdini had hidden her before he'd ghosted past the Far Edge Club to the exit, the poison that was killing him, and the murder of Le Saphir Mortal.

"There's a few details I need to wrap up," the magician admitted to his manager.

꒰ᴑꝊꝊꙶ

The Marquis sipped a fresh young Chablis and scowled. "Say what you like," he complained to Lascalle, "I can still taste the American in this."[12]

"Americans can leave a bad taste in the mouth," agreed the lawyer.

---

12   From 1863, the classic French vine-stocks that were a national pride were systematically destroyed by Phylloxera vastatrix, the grape louse. Ancient vintages from Chablis to Champagne, Beaujolais to St Émilion were threatened with extinction. Salvation came by grafting French vines onto Californian rootstocks – the American plants were resistant to the parasite. Hence all modern French wines have American antecedents. Some French oenophiles still prefer not to be reminded of this.

De Confontaine set the wine aside. "Where is he?" The aristocrat felt no need to define the article of his enquiry.

"Houdini escaped the Pump Room with Mademoiselle Sheffield. Le Sapphire was not so fortunate. She has sparkled her last."

"She was beginning to lose her lustre. You have not, however, answered my enquiry as to M. Houdini's location."

"He and the *fille* vanished into the labyrinth," Lascalle explained. "He emerged from the water pipes by the stone bridge. He rendered two of the hunters unconscious at that point and escaped into the mine shafts."

"Then he will be coming here," the Marquis concluded. "He knows that only I possess the specific for the toxin in his blood. He has perhaps an hour before it begins to sap his strength, two before he is pain-wracked and unable to move, a mere day thereafter before death. He will seek me out."

"The stair-traps are prepared," Lascalle promised. "The pressure plates are primed. Their blowdarts are newly laced with venom. The chamber beyond now contains over one hundred venomous reptiles. The upper door is armed to release mustard gas when it is opened. Even the ingenious M. Houdini may find his ingenuity growing thin at that point."

"Oh, I think he's plenty ingenious," Harry Houdini said. He leaned in the doorway, slipping on a set of brass knuckles.

Lascalle gasped and stepped back. He knocked into the table, shattering the glass of Chablis across the marble floor.

The Marquis quirked an eyebrow. "I am most impressed," he confessed. "And intrigued."

Houdini saw no reason to explain his tricks to the enemy, but he was always happy to divert his audience's attention. "Dumb of you to set a trap your quarry can just walk round," he pointed out. "You seemed pretty keen that I head back here to get that antidote from you. But there are plenty of other ways to the surface than up the stairs under your house."

"You exited another way and entered my mansion above ground," de Confontaine reasoned. "Easier to break in from outside than brave my gauntlet from below. *Tres bien!*"

Houdini was in no mood for banter. "You have to answer for the death of Marie-Anne Legris," he warned.

Lascalle broke and fled for the other door. "*Attendez! Attendez!*" he called for aid.

Houdini's diversion had worked. The lawyer ran straight into Martin Beck's revolver-butt. "Negotiate that," spat the manager to the troublesome attorney.

"May I enquire what has become of the *délicieux* Mademoiselle Diane?" the Marquis asked. "I have some very specific intentions for her when you are destroyed. I doubt that you could have slipped past my guards with her trailing behind you, so you have clearly concealed her somewhere in the tunnels below."

Houdini didn't like how quickly de Confontaine followed his thinking. He dragged the Marquis of his chair. "It's over, buster. Miss Sheffield will be giving such testimony about you to the Prefect of Police that all your high-ranking buddies put together won't save you. And if that doesn't work then she'll talk to the British Consul. And if that won't do the trick I'll be on to the American embassy as well." He shook the Marquis like a rat. "And if that fails, I've always got these here brass knuckles."

"I think you have some antidote that belongs to my client," Beck told de Confontaine.

"In the cabinet," the Marquis answered.

Beck moved to open the carved antique before Houdini could cry "Stop!" The manager wasn't able to halt in time. As the hinged cabinet door opened fractionally it emitted a mechanical click.

"Don't move an inch!" Houdini warned Beck. "What's he triggered, De Confontaine?"

"An explosive device," the Marquis shrugged. "Not too large. It will claim his hand, perhaps scar him for life and blind him, but he may well survive it. If the cupboard door moves even a fraction, open or closed, then you will need a new minion."

Beck didn't move, even to reply to the aristocrat's insult. "Houdini…?"

The showman hurled the Marquis back into his chair and turned to help his friend. The cabinet was only three feet high, a marquetry delight in teak and beech. A single panel opened at the front, and it was to that which the incendiary mechanism had been attached.

Houdini noted the ticking from inside the furniture. The Marquis loved his clockwork. In addition to a movement trigger there was also a spring-wound timer.

Houdini turned back to de Confontaine. "Where's the off button?"

But the Marquis was no longer in his chair. Somehow, incredibly, he had vanished.

"He really is the Devil," breathed Beck. "You'll just have to find the stop button yourself, Houdini. Quickly would be good."

De Confontaine's voice seemed to come from nowhere. "Why would I allow such an easy solution? There is no way to stop the device, M. Houdini.

You have three minutes to abandon your man and get clear – or to follow me as I descend to find the lovely Diane Sheffield! *Au revoir!*"

The Marquis had escaped.

"Houdini!" Beck prompted. "Could you please defuse this?"

The showman nodded. "Although this is really when I should re-negotiate my contract," he pointed out. "But since you brought those revellers to overwhelm the guards waiting at my chosen exit point I suppose I owe you one."

"I'd say so. Why didn't you tell me what you were planning?"

"I didn't want you at risk."

Beck looked down at his hand on the cabinet door. "So much for that," he snorted.

Houdini pulled the tiny phial of acid and broke it down the reverse of the furniture. The liquid hissed on the lacquered wood and dissolved a hole in the back of the cupboard.

"How did you know where I'd be coming out anyway?" Houdini wondered.

"Come now. Knowing where one's client is and what he is up to is half an agent's job. And you always like to rehearse your stunts where possible."

"You followed me yesterday afternoon."

"And decided I needed to protect my investment when young Sheffield confessed he'd been ordered to inveigle you into this all along."

Houdini reached a hand through the hole in the cabinet's rear and easily disabled the trap. "I have to go," he told the released Beck. "The Marquis correctly deduced that I hid Diane in the ossuary below. I need to get to her before he does. Can I rely on you to involve the authorities up here and bring holy hell down on the Far Edge Club now?"

"Oh, you can rely on me," Beck agreed vengefully.

Houdini took the ampoule from the cabinet and injected the anti-toxin into his arm. He examined the fireplace by the Marquis' chair, where a twist of a decoration opened a secret door. A tiny chamber behind headed another stairway to the catacombs of Paris.

"Then it's time for the last act," Houdini said.

~⟊~

The hunters of the Far Edge Club knew the catacombs well. Once the Marquis told them where to look it was less than half an hour before they located Diane Sheffield and dragged her out before de Confontaine himself.

The Marquis found her in the old burial tunnels, where six million skulls were stacked in high walls and remarkable arrangements. In the light of the burning braziers the sadistic aristocrat looked more Satanic than ever.

"I believe you should scream now," de Confontaine advised the English girl. "It will be good practice for later and it will speed M. Houdini to this meeting."

"That won't be necessary," Houdini assured him. The showman emerged from the shadows beside a column of ribs. "I'm here. This seemed like a good place for our showdown."

Diane ripped herself free of her assailants and fled to the American. "They found me! I'm sorry."

"No, you did fine," Houdini assured her. "You volunteered to be bait and it worked perfectly. He's here and so are we."

De Confontaine frowned, suddenly uncertain. "M'sieu, you are surrounded by your enemies. You are far underground, away from the public ossuary passageways that are displayed to the morbid droolings of the masses, without help or hope. The entrance sign to this place warns that this is the Empire of Death. For you that shall be the case."

"The thrill of death's closeness," Houdini recognised. He looked at effete masked figures that flanked the triumphant nobleman. "The approach of the Far Edge."

"Just so. Diane, your paladin has failed. Once again you are wagered and lost. There is no salvation for you now. Your horror and our pleasure will be in equal proportion. M. Houdini, you have afforded us a most memorable entertainment. Your bones will join the others here but your memory will be honoured by the players of our little society."

"Behind me, Diane," Houdini warned as the Marquis stepped forward, lifted his gun, and aimed.

"No last words?" de Confontaine mocked. "Perhaps, 'I should have studied Robert-Houdin more carefully'?"

He closed his finger on his trigger and fired.

Houdini fell backwards violently and sprawled on the floor. Diane screamed.

Etienne-Louis de Confontaine laughed.

And then Houdini sat up. He drew back his lips and spit out the bullet trapped between his teeth.

"That… is not possible!" breathed the Marquis.

It wasn't. Houdini had palmed the bullets from de Confontaine's gun as he'd manhandled the aristocrat out of his chair in the mansion; he'd substituted blanks instead. Slipping a round into his mouth as his fell had been child's play. But there was no need to tell the Marquis any of that – not now Houdini had landed near the concealed wires he'd placed earlier!

"Showtime," the showman snarled.

Diane Sheffield was exactly where he needed her, away from the charges he'd planted in his underground explorations yesterday. Houdini hadn't known what part of the rambling underworld he'd be hunted through, but there was one distinctive part that was easily accessible to him beforehand, the bone tunnels themselves. Hiding Diane there had drawn the Marquis to prepared territory.

As the copper wires touched in Houdini's hand the first explosions began. Bright firework flashes flared from the skulls' mouths, painting the boneyard in eerie green light. Smoke welled from nowhere, coiling like angry spirits around the suddenly-frightened clubmen. Screaming squibs filled the caves with the outrage of the damned.

The Marquis looked around him, surprised, suddenly out of control. The game was no longer his.

Houdini joined the other wires. "For Le Saphir," he said.

Larger detonations began. Antique walls of bones toppled from their rest to spill down over the Far Edge Club. The men who wanted the thrill of death's nearness were slammed down under the weight of thousands of falling skeletons. The rattle of the descending dead seemed like vengeful chatter.

The Marquis was right under the central bone arch. He looked up, shocked and horrified, as the charnel weight collapsed on him – and the roof above it!

Houdini covered Diane with his body as the aristocrat and his cronies were buried by the relicts of death, the inhabitants of a world beyond the furthest edge.

The rain of corpses ended at last. Silence returned to the tunnels of the dead.

The wager was done.

~9QC~

Many rich men were recovered dead or alive from the tunnel collapse. The Marquis de Confontaine's body was never found.

~9QC~

The Gare du Nord railway platform was washed with steam from the waiting cross-channel locomotive. Houdini shook hands with Sheffield and received a kiss from Diane.

"I apologise for all the trouble I've caused," Sheffield said. "I'll do what you said, Mr Houdini, go home wiser and do better."

"I shall never forget your kindness," the English girl told the magician. "You saved my life. You did not also have to clear my brother's debts and allow us to return home in style."

"It was the Marquis' money," shrugged Houdini. "We still turned a profit and snagged another headline. All in a day's work."

Beck, who received a percentage, nodded happily. "And the Prefect de Police is finally acting. The Far Edge Club is no longer welcome in Paris."

Houdini watched the Sheffields board the express. "Now we have a show to open," he said to Beck. "What do you think we can do to *really* catch these Parisians' attention?"

THE END

WHY HOUDINI HAD TO VISIT PARIS

F in-de-siecle Paris was a remarkable place. Less than thirty years before, the city had been sieged and occupied by Prussian troops. Many people still living remembered eating cats, dogs, and the animals from the zoo to survive the famine. The City of Lights had endured a hundred and thirty years of turmoil since the French Revolution and the Terror, through the rise and fall of Napoleon (twice), the return of the monarchy (twice), the Commune, invasion and hardship. And somehow, after all of this, it had become the focus of a new century, new technology, new morality, new culture.

Rising from the dark past, the beginning of France's *belle époque* started with creators like Mallarmé and Debussy, with the rise of artistic symbolism, and in works like Oscar Wilde's *Salomé*. Growing industrialisation led to the rapid population rise that changed outlying villages like Montmartre and Montparnasse into crowded low-rent suburbs that became hothouses of crime, violence, vice – and counter-culture. The first flower-power revolution began in the shadow of the infamous Moulin Rouge.

"Houdini and the Catacombs of Paris" places a fictionalised version of the famous showman in a fictionalised 1902 capital of France. In each case the broad strokes are there. Like an impressionist painting the effect is in the feeling not the detail. But some elements are perhaps worth a closer examination.

In 1900, Paris hosted a world fair. The gateway to that amazing event was Gustave Eiffel's remarkable "candlestick", the controversial tower that took his name. Originally intended as a temporary structure, it was then the world's tallest building. Its construction divided Paris into fervent partisans and rabid opponents. Thomas Edison was a great admirer. Architect Charles Garnier and writer Alexandre Dumas led the opposition. Its greatest critic, Guy de Maupassant, allegedly dined there every day since it was the only place he could look from the window and not see it on the skyline.

The Tower somehow became the symbol of new France – shocking, controversial, stylish, brazen, and impossible to ignore.

The same is true of the entertainment industry that grew up alongside the artistic, social, and economic developments of the city. Napoleon had established licensed "tolerance houses" to regulate the spread of venereal disease amongst his troops, but by the turn of the 19th century many Parisian brothers were lavish expensive affairs, meeting places of the noble and the famous. Their influence in turn promoted the kind of club and show nightlife that gave the world the can-can and the hunkadolla.

And that led to the Grand Guignol spectacles of shock and horror that took their name from the theatre where the style emerged. France took the sensibility-shaking headlines of the British *Police News Illustrated* and the penny dreadful publications like *Varney the Vampire* and showed them on stage. Blood, gore, and nudity were essential parts of the show. The cast depicted murderers, blackmailers, prostitutes, violated maidens, mad scientists, and perverted butchers, a distorted mirror of the grim underbelly in the shadow cast by brilliant Parisian society.

And under the dazzle and the darkness lurked death.

L'Ossuaire Municipal is a small part of a massive set of underground tunnels beneath the city. Between 1786 and 1788 old stone quarries were filled with the bones of six million skeletons displaced from the "charniers" or bone-houses of the overcrowded Saints Innocents cemetery and others. From 1810, site inspector Louis-Étienne Héricart de Thury transformed the underground caverns into planned and visitable sepulchres. Skulls and femurs were arranged into artistic walls and columns, beside such tombstones and cemetery decorations as had survived the 1789 revolution.

The mausoleum was open to the public from 1867. It rapidly became a tourist attraction, although only a part of the system was accessible. The tunnels disappear off into other old workings, Napoleonic sewers, medieval passages, and even older cave systems.

New age Paris had dark roots.

All of this offers an ideal setting for Harry Houdini, that vigorous adventurer showman from the New World which was likewise forging ahead into the twentieth century. America was a very different place to France; it was inventing itself after an age of pioneering. France was redefining itself after an epoch of chaos. The French had given the United States the Statue of Liberty and New Orleans (well, they sold the U.S. New Orleans). America exported a brash can-do optimism that sent its citizens burning through the Old World like fireworks.

The contrasts shaped and informed the present story. Houdini personifies American ingenuity, that sense of the liberty, equality, and fraternity that the French had once hoped for before being dragged into bloody tyranny, war, poverty, and disgrace then painfully climbing out again. Paris is the sophisticated whirlpool that clean-cut Kentucky country boys are warned to avoid by their worried mothers. "How you gonna keep 'em down on the farm/ Now that they've seen Par-ee?"

So Houdini needed to meet an adversary that personified the sinister ancient power that still persisted behind the shining new age. The aristos had reclaimed France and made it their playground. A wicked Marquis seemed in order.

And there needed to be a point of contention. A third party had to play the role of innocent abroad, the victim threatened by the wicked city. The naïve Sheffields got the part.

The rest followed naturally: American know-how and vigour versus ancient privilege and vice against a glittering cityscape backdrop, ending in the waiting tombs of the dead.

I.A. WATSON enjoys telling stories but hates writing paragraphs about himself for pages like this one. He nurses his compulsive writing habits with the help of occasional novels such as his award-nominated four-volume *Robin Hood* series, *St George and the Dragon* Books 1 and 2, *The Transdimensional Travel Company,* and *Labours of Hercules,* or by contributing stories to anthologies such as *Sherlock Holmes: Consulting Detective* volumes 1-7, *Zeppelin Tales,* and *Legends of New Pulp.* His new novel *Holmes and Houdini,* which follows on from his story in the present volume, is out soon from Airship 27. A full list of his publications, free samples, and some complete short stories are available at http://www.chillwater.org.uk/writing/

MAGICIAN'S RAZOR
BY ROMAN LEARY

The man's name was Hans Ulrich, but he came billed as "Ulrich the Uncanny." He was a wily old duffer, with a crooked smile and a twinkle in his eye that said *mischief*. Beck didn't care for him, but it was clear that Houdini had taken a shine to the man.

"More coffee, sir?" asked a waiter as he stopped by their table.

"None for me, thank you," Beck replied. Houdini passed as well, but Ulrich took a refill, as did Monsieur Lachance.

"So, Houdini," said Lachance, "what do you think of the food here on the Nord Express?"

"It was a delicious meal," Houdini said with a smile. "You have every right to be proud of the accommodations on this line."

Lachance beamed. "May I quote you on that? My fellow board members will surely give me a bonus if I secure an endorsement from the Master Mystifier."

Beck spoke up before Houdini could reply. "I'm sure we would be willing to discuss terms if you could provide Mr. Houdini with a formal proposal for…"

"Oh, for Heaven's sake, Beck," Houdini interrupted with a good-natured laugh. "Put away your manager hat for a while. Can't you just relax and enjoy the ride?"

Beck sighed and lifted his hands in mock surrender. "All right, all right," he said. "No more business talk tonight."

"Does that mean we can't discuss magic?" Ulrich asked.

"Oh, there's nothing I'd rather talk about," Houdini said.

"Careful, Herr Ulrich," Beck said, "or you'll still be sitting here when they serve breakfast before we pull into Berlin."

"My friend is only half-joking," Houdini said. "You'll probably get tired of the subject long before I will."

The old man chuckled. "Not likely," he said. "I am a great raconteur."

"I'm glad to hear it," Houdini said. "You have no idea how pleased I was to learn you were on this train. It's an honor to meet one of Europe's great practitioners of card manipulation."

"Former practitioner, I'm afraid," Ulrich said. He was about to say more when he was interrupted by a delicate feminine hand falling upon his shoulder.

The hand belonged to a statuesque blonde in a light blue dress who was standing in the aisle, swaying with the movement of the train. "I beg your pardon," the woman said. "I did not mean to grab you. It's just that I lost my balance for a moment."

"Think nothing of it, my dear," Ulrich said. "I'm always happy to assist a beautiful young...um...I..."

Ulrich stared up at the woman as if he had inadvertently made some dreadful faux-pas. Beck followed the magician's gaze and saw what had unsettled the old man. The woman was blind. Her pale, clouded eyes rolled in their sockets, as if seeking an elusive light in the darkness.

The woman tilted her head and smiled down at Ulrich. "I can tell that you're embarrassed," she said. "Please don't be. Just because I'm blind doesn't mean I don't appreciate compliments. My name is Anna Richter, by the way. May I ask to whom I am speaking?"

Ulrich stood up and took the woman's hand. "I am known as Ulrich the Uncanny," he said, with just a touch of melodrama.

"Ah, the famous magician!" said Fräulein Richter. "This is quite an honor."

Ulrich looked as if he had been granted a knighthood. "The honor is mine," he said. "Is there any way I can be of service to you?"

"Would you be so kind as to assist me back to my compartment? I indulged in a second glass of wine with my meal and I'm afraid it may have affected me more than I realized. I've already misplaced my change purse and Heaven knows what clumsy thing I'll do next."

"I would be glad to help you, dear lady, of course." Ulrich turned to his companions. "Pardon me, gentlemen. I shall return momentarily."

Beck watched them toddle down the aisle and then glanced at Houdini. "Romance in bloom?" he said.

"Don't be ridiculous," Houdini said. "He's old enough to be her grandfather."

"Love does not recognize age," Lachance said, winking at Beck. "For my own part, I believe our 'uncanny' friend is already smitten, and I can hardly blame him. Fräulein Richter is not only a beautiful woman; she also has a delightful personality."

"You know her?" Houdini asked.

"I was coming back from Hanover last week when she boarded in Cologne. We talked a little then. She was very friendly, and charmed everyone who met her. I'm sure this trip has been no different."

Beck was intrigued. "Is she traveling alone?"

"Yes," said Lachance. "She has no qualms about asking for help, but she doesn't seem to require it very often. I think the woman is utterly fearless."

Charming. Beautiful. Fearless. Beck nodded appreciatively. He hoped he would have occasion to speak to Anna Richter again before the journey's end. She was easily the most interesting of their fellow passengers. Then again, numerically speaking, she had little competition. The dining car was sparsely populated, as was the rest of the train. Beck commented on this to Lachance.

"It is unusual to have so few passengers," the Belgian said, "but not unheard of. This is a special express to Berlin. If there were more scheduled stops, we would have more people aboard."

At that moment, a door opened at the end of the car and Ulrich entered, smiling from ear-to-ear. "Marvelous woman," he said as he rejoined them. "If I were twenty years younger…"

"You used the phrase, *former practitioner*," Houdini said.

Ulrich blinked at him. "I beg your pardon?"

"Earlier, when I complimented you on your skills as a card manipulator, you spoke as if you could no longer do it."

Ulrich kept his smile, but it took on a rueful quality. He held up his hands. The fingers were long and delicate, but Beck thought he could detect an abnormal swelling in the knuckles…

"Arthritis," Houdini said softly.

"I'm afraid so," Ulrich replied. "It's getting worse every day. I haven't completely lost my abilities, but they are fading fast. I'm sad to say that Ulrich the Uncanny will soon be making his final exit."

"I'm very sorry to hear that," Houdini said. "If there is anything I can do to help, please let me know."

Beck knew this wasn't mere rhetoric. Houdini had a soft spot for old magicians, and would give the shirt off his back to one in need.

"As a matter of fact," Ulrich said, "there *is* something you can do. It will cost you nothing, and it will mean the world to me."

"Name it," Houdini said.

"You could accept a challenge."

Houdini grinned. "That's how I've made my reputation. I assume you wish to test my skills as an escape artist. What's it to be? Custom-made manacles? A submerged coffin?"

"No, no, nothing so baroque. I wish to challenge your skills as thinker. More than that, I wish to challenge your very beliefs!"

"I'm listening," Houdini said.

"It is well-known that you are skeptical of mediums and their methods," Ulrich said.

"I am," Houdini replied.

"Do you discount the existence of spirits altogether?"

"I do not," Houdini said. "In fact, I would love to see irrefutable evidence of their reality. It would be the most amazing discovery in the history of the world. Unfortunately, evidence, *real* evidence, is something the spiritualists sorely lack."

"Well said!" Ulrich exclaimed. "You have come directly to the heart of the matter, the very reason why we are here."

"The reason we're here? I'm not sure I'm following you."

"Our meeting tonight is no accident, Herr Houdini. I made a close study of your itinerary, and I knew you would be aboard this train."

"So you made arrangements to join me. I don't know whether to be flattered or alarmed."

Ulrich laughed. "Perhaps both."

"And why did you go to all this trouble?"

"So that you could bear witness to the crowning achievement of my career. Tonight, I, Ulrich the Uncanny, will prove beyond the shadow of a doubt that the dead can speak to the living!"

There was a long pause after Ulrich's pronouncement. Beck broke the silence before it became uncomfortable. "How exactly do you propose to do that?"

"You shall see," Ulrich said with a little smirk that Beck found rather childish.

"Let me get this straight," Houdini said, "you're claiming that you can actually communicate with spirits?"

"I claim that you will not be able to prove otherwise."

"Carefully put," Beck said dryly.

"And if I can't," Houdini said, "then what? What do you hope to gain?"

Ulrich's face took on a somber cast. "One last triumph before I fade into obscurity."

"Do you really need me for that?"

"Perhaps our friend here put it best," Ulrich said, nodding toward Lachance. "I want the endorsement of the Master Mystifier."

"Very well," Houdini said. "I accept your challenge. Beck, do you have pen and paper close at hand?"

"I do," Beck said. He retrieved a notepad and a shiny new Montblanc from his valise.

"Take this down: I, Harry Houdini, do solemnly affirm that Hans Ulrich, also known as Ulrich the Uncanny, has produced an effect which I can neither explain nor re-create. He is either an authentic spiritual medium, or the greatest magician I have ever seen."

Beck transcribed the words. "Anything else?"

Houdini shook his head and looked at Ulrich. "If you can make good on your claims, I will sign and date that statement, and it will be yours to do with as you will."

Ulrich rubbed his hands together. "Excellent," he said. "Let us begin."

⁓つ◯⌒

Lachance stood in front of the door leading to the sleeping car, tapping his glass with a fork. "Ladies and gentlemen," he said, "may I have your attention please."

The passengers complied, their conversations dying as they turned their eyes on the stocky Belgian.

"My name is Claude Lachance. I am on the board of directors of the *Compagnie Internationale des Wagons-Lits*, which operates this train. Tonight, I am very pleased to offer you a surprise entertainment which I am sure you will be telling your friends about for many years to come, a performance…"

"Demonstration," Ulrich corrected.

"I beg your pardon, a *demonstration* of…of…"

"Spiritual mediumship," Ulrich said.

"Indeed, a demonstration of this remarkable phenomenon by the celebrated Ulrich the Uncanny!"

An appreciative murmur ran through the dining car. It seemed the magician was not unknown to his fellow passengers.

"Before we begin," Lachance continued, "Herr Ulrich has asked that no one enter or leave during his per…his demonstration. Is there anyone who would like to go before we begin?"

No one moved from their seat.

"Very well," said Lachance. "Our conductor, Monsieur Roche, will make sure we are not interrupted. Anyone he has to turn away from the dining car will be compensated for their inconvenience, although I am sure they will forever curse their luck for missing this extraordinary opportunity."

This remark was rewarded with a few polite chuckles. Lachance beamed as if he had brought down the house.

"Now," he said, "without further ado, I give you...*Ulrich the Uncanny!*"

Lachance resumed his seat as Ulrich came to the head of the car. The magician's eyes glittered as he surveyed his audience, and a look of serene confidence settled over his face. Beck noted with interest that the man seemed to grow younger as he slipped into his stage persona. No longer a frail old man in the twilight of his career, Ulrich was now the very picture of a performer at the peak of his powers. The spotlight could have that effect, sometimes.

"My fellow passengers," Ulrich began, "it is an honor and a privilege to stand before you this evening. As my friend Monsieur Lachance has pointed out, I am not here in my capacity as a master of prestidigitation, but rather as an apostle; a traveler on a path to enlightenment upon which, for a brief time, I will invite you to join me."

Beck smiled. This was good patter, delivered in the rich, sonorous tones of a practiced seducer.

"Tonight," Ulrich continued, "before your very eyes, I will open my heart and mind to the eternal, and the eternal shall speak through me. I shall become a vessel for the spirits, and they will fill me with intimate knowledge...about all of *you*." He made an expansive gesture that took in the whole of the car. There was a feminine gasp, and someone laughed nervously.

"Now, my friends, please grant me complete silence as I reach out to the realms beyond..."

Ulrich closed his eyes and turned up his palms. The only sound in the car was the iron rumbling of the train.

"Yes," Ulrich said, "the door is opening. I see the light of the other side. I hear voices calling out. They are calling my name. They are saying..."

"You're letting in the cold air," some wag muttered. There were a few stifled chortles, but Ulrich maintained his concentration.

"They are saying...surrender yourself, that we may communicate with the living."

Ulrich stiffened and threw back his head, as if in the grip of a seizure. There was a hiss as he made a sharp intake of breath through his clenched teeth. Lachance, clearly alarmed, rose from his seat. He reached for Ulrich, but the magician batted away his hand.

"Do not lay hands upon my person," Ulrich said, his voice deeper and more resonant than it had been a moment earlier. He opened his eyes and fixed Lachance with an imperious gaze.

"Herr Ulrich?" Lachance said. "Are you quite..."

"He is perfectly fine," Ulrich said.

Lachance was nonplused. "He?"

"The one called Ulrich," the magician said. "He has retreated into the ether so that I might come forth. I am Den, son of Queen Merneith, King of the Two Lands."

Beck and Houdini shared a glance.

"Do you doubt me, men of the world?" Ulrich said.

Beck turned and saw that Ulrich was staring directly at him. He felt his face flush.

Ulrich slowly raised his arm and pointed a long finger. "Come forth, both of you."

"I don't think…" Beck started, but Houdini grabbed his arm and pulled him down the aisle to the front of the car.

They stopped about an arm's length from Ulrich. "What would you have us do?" Houdini asked.

"Stand beside me, so that I may steady myself. I have not worn flesh for thousands of years, and the feeling is very strange to me."

Houdini gave Beck an almost imperceptible shrug. Beck took the cue. He and Houdini took up positions on the left and right of the old magician. Ulrich placed a hand on each of their shoulders. The grip was firm, and Beck winced slightly as the fingertips pressed into his flesh.

Ulrich turned to Houdini. "You are a soothsayer, are you not?"

Houdini kept a straight face. "I am a showman."

"Look upon these faces, showman, and tell me what you see."

Houdini regarded the audience. "I see six men, two women, and a young girl."

"And what do you know about them?"

"They are passengers on an express train to Berlin."

"Is that all?" Ulrich sniffed. "Shall I tell you what *I* know?"

"By all means."

"There is someone here," Ulrich said, his voice registering deeper and increasing in volume, "who has recently lost a beloved wife. He sat by her bed day and night while she died of a wasting disease. He held her hand while she lingered in agony. He wept as she called out his name in her fitful slumber."

"*Mein Gott*," someone whispered. Beck's eye fell on a stocky, balding man with a gray walrus moustache. The man was pale and trembling, and a monocle fell from one of his widened eyes. The effect would have been comical, if the poor man had not looked so utterly stricken.

Ulrich did not shift his gaze from Houdini. "I bring that man glad tidings," he said. "His wife is safe and happy on the other side. She is no longer in pain, and she looks forward to the day she will see him again."

Beck thought the stocky man was about to speak, but the fellow was too overcome, and he sat shaking, a single hand held over his eyes.

Beck looked at Houdini, but he couldn't catch his friend's eye. Houdini was focused entirely on Ulrich. There was an odd look on his face, and it took Beck a moment to identify it.

He's disappointed, Beck thought. *He thinks this carny stuff is beneath the old man's dignity. Probably feels sorry for the widower, too. I never should have let him agree to this.*

Perhaps Ulrich, or Den, King of the Two Lands, saw the disappointment, too, because he turned from Houdini and closed his eyes. "There is someone here," he said, "who lost a child in an accident. The little boy was learning to ride horses. He fell…"

"Henri!" a young woman cried out. She rose from her chair, but a young man sitting beside her, Beck guessed the fellow was her husband, caught her shoulder and gently pulled her back down.

Ulrich bit his lower lip, and Beck saw a bead of sweat run down the old man's face. "I bring you glad tidings," he said, his voice slightly unsteady. "The boy wishes for me to tell you that he is happy and whole and he loves you very much…"

"Oh, my little boy," the woman wailed, and her grief seemed to crash into Beck like a tangible thing, a breaking wave from an ocean of misery.

Okay, enough is enough, Beck thought. He opened his mouth to speak, but he was silenced by a sudden squeeze of Ulrich's hand. The old man's eyes snapped open, and the corners of his mouth lifted in a sardonic smile.

"Ah-ha," he said, "and what's this? I believe there is a thief aboard this train."

"I beg your pardon?" Lachance said.

Now, he speaks up, Beck thought, rolling his eyes. Apparently it was okay to tear people's hearts out, but slanderous accusations were another matter altogether.

"Yes, indeed," Ulrich said. "I shall not name you, but you know who you are. You should be ashamed of your disgraceful behavior."

Beck scanned the audience, but if there was a guilty face, he couldn't spot it.

"You have until midnight to return what you have stolen," Ulrich said. "Undo what you have done, and you will be spared my wrath. I give you the word of Den, King of the Two Lands."

"Now see here," Lachance said in a low voice. "If you have knowledge of…"

"Wait!" Ulrich gasped. "There is a cry from the darkness…A lost soul calls out to me…I hear a single word…*Murder!*"

A silence heavy as August heat fell over the car. Beck could almost hear the sound of his own heartbeat.

"Murder," Ulrich repeated. "Yes, someone in this car is a murderer!"

"Who?" Beck asked. He felt an odd mix of trepidation and excitement. Ulrich was really playing with fire. How far was the man prepared to go?

"The voice is faint," the magician said. "It has been weakened by the manner in which it was wrenched from this plane…the savagery…the ultimate betrayal…"

Ulrich's features twisted into a rictus of pain. Tears flowed from his eyes.

"I must go to them," he said. "I must go, and then I will return. I will return to you at midnight. I will return…*with a name.*"

"This has gone far enough," Lachance said. "You're making serious allegations and I for one think that…"

Ulrich fainted.

⟡

The old magician came around about five minutes later. "What happened?" he asked, clutching his head as if recovering from a hangover. They had seated him at a table near the front of the car. The other passengers were crowding around, craning their necks at Ulrich, muttering darkly. The tension in the air was palpable, and Beck wished Lachance or the conductor would tell everyone to go back to their compartments.

"You were possessed by the spirit of a man called Den," Houdini said in a matter-of-fact tone. "He was apparently some sort of Egyptian prince. It was pretty amazing."

"Was it? What did I…What did *he* say?"

"He poured salt in the wounds of some recently bereaved people," Houdini said.

Beck saw Ulrich's jaw clench. "Is that all?"

"He accused someone of theft, and someone else of murder."

Ulrich looked genuinely surprised. "Murder?"

"Yes," Houdini said, staring into Ulrich's eyes. "He seemed to be unsure of the culprit's identity, but he promised to return at midnight with a name."

"Then I had best be prepared," Ulrich said. He stood up and straightened his coat.

"Prepared to face charges for slander!" Lachance said. "What the hell are you playing at? I thought you were going to do some harmless tricks, not turn the train upside-down!"

Now, that would have been something to see, Beck thought.

"I have not performed any so-called tricks," Ulrich said. "What you have seen tonight is an authentic instance of contact with the beyond, and if Den said he would name a murderer at midnight, then *it will happen*."

A tall man in a tweed suit shouldered between Beck and Houdini. "Herr Ulrich," the man said, his voice crisp and business-like, "if you have knowledge of a crime, I insist that you share it with me immediately."

Lachance didn't welcome the interruption. "And just who the devil are you?"

"I am *Hauptleuten* Friedrich Nagel of the *Königliche Schutzmannschaft zu Berlin*."

Beck sent Houdini a questioning glance.

"Captain Nagel, here, is with the Berlin Police," Houdini said.

"That is correct," Nagel said, "and I will not tolerate someone playing games when it comes to murder. Now, Herr Ulrich, I will put it to you plainly, is there a killer on this train or is this merely some ill-advised prank. Speak up, sir!"

Ulrich wasn't cowed. "No pranks and no games," he said. "Den is a being of his word. Wait and you will see."

Nagel didn't seem very impressed. "And will this ghost offer evidence to support his accusations?"

"I suppose we shall find out at the stroke of twelve," Ulrich replied.

"What about my wife?" a deep voice bellowed. The bald man with the walrus moustache pushed aside Lachance and glowered down at Ulrich. "My name is Albert Kalb. My wife's name was Theresa. How did you know about her? About the way she died?"

"Sir, it wasn't me," Ulrich said. "I was merely a vessel through which…"

Kalb grabbed Ulrich by the lapels and snatched him to his feet. "Listen to me, you little bastard! I'm not falling for any of that nonsense! I want the truth and I want it now!"

A small woman grabbed the bald man's arm. Kalb was so lost in his fury that Beck feared he might strike her. Beck was about to intervene, but then he saw a transformation in Kalb's features. The apoplectic rage abruptly fled, and was replaced with something like pity.

"Please," the woman said, her voice choked with sobs. "Please, stop. Let me speak to him, I beg you."

Kalb relented. He released Ulrich and quietly withdrew, but not without giving the magician a venomous look that promised their conversation would continue.

"Sir," the woman said to Ulrich, "my name is Emilie Cloutier. You said something about a boy killed in a riding accident."

Ulrich swallowed. "Dear lady," he said "my memories of what took place while I was in the trance are hazy at best…"

"Can't you tell me more about the boy? His name is Henri. My little boy…"

The woman's husband stepped up behind her. His features were drawn and his eyes were rimmed with red. "This isn't the time, Emilie," he said softly. "We'll talk with Herr Ulrich later."

"But, Michel, I have to know…"

"Later, Emilie."

Emilie Cloutier, now weeping uncontrollably, buried her face in her husband's chest. Holding her close, the man turned a baleful eye on Ulrich. "If you have trifled with our grief," he said, "I promise that you will regret it."

Lachance spoke up. "Monsieur Cloutier, please let me apologize on behalf of…"

"You'll regret it, too," Cloutier said, and he guided his wife out of the dining car.

Lachance closed his eyes and pinched the bridge of his nose. "Could this possibly get any worse?" he muttered.

As if in reply, a portly matron with an adolescent girl in tow appeared and began to wag a finger in his face. "Monsieur Lachance, my name is Claudette Debans, and I want you to know that my granddaughter has been traumatized by this experience! Thoroughly traumatized!"

Beck looked at the girl. She was a pretty little brunette with large, dark eyes. She looked apprehensive, maybe a little embarrassed, but not traumatized. He glanced at Houdini, and the magician appeared to be studying the girl quite closely. Beck wondered why.

"You will be hearing from my advocate," the woman continued. "You and your board!"

Lachance sighed heavily. "Madame, I assure you…" but by then he was talking to her back. His lip curled and he wheeled on Ulrich. "You damned charlatan!" he snarled. "Do you see what you've brought down on me! I'd like to wring your scrawny neck!"

"Please, stop. Let me speak to him, I beg you."

"I am *not* a charlatan!" Ulrich shouted, and everyone in the car fell silent and still. "I said I would open a door to the afterlife, and that is exactly what I have done. I did not promise that it would be pleasant or amusing. If some of you have been distressed by what you have seen, I am sorry, but I do not choose what the spirits elect to share."

Lachance was exasperated. "Oh, come now! Can we please abandon this pretense?"

"Pretense?" Ulrich said, his face flushed with anger. "If this is all pretense, then how did I know about Theresa Kalb, or Henri Cloutier?"

"How should I know?" Lachance said. He turned to Houdini. "Is it possible that he's telling the truth? Did he really channel the spirit of some ancient Egyptian?"

Every eye in the car fell on Houdini.

"Harry?" Beck said softly.

"Herr Ulrich has not yet earned my endorsement," Houdini said, his gaze fixed firmly on the old magician. "However, I am keeping an open mind. I'm very interested to see what will happen at midnight."

An almost imperceptible smile pulled at the corner of Ulrich's mouth. He turned to Lachance. "I am going to my compartment to rest and recuperate," he said. "I will return to this room in..." he consulted a pocket watch "...three hours. I invite everyone here to join me at that time, so they can watch as the spirits unmask a murderer."

"My God," Lachance said. His voice was barely above a whisper, but everyone in the dining car could hear his words. "You really mean it."

"Indeed, I do," Ulrich said, "and then, by Heaven, everyone on this train will know why I am called *the Uncanny*."

He cast a brief, defiant glance at the other passengers, then pushed past Lachance and went for the door.

Lachance immediately followed after him. "Wait! Please! Let us discuss this!"

As they exited the car, there seemed to be a release in the tension, and Beck could have sworn that he heard the other passengers draw a single collective breath.

"Well," Beck said, "what do we do now?"

Houdini smiled. "It seems that we have a little time to kill," he said. "I'm going to return to my table and request another serving of that delicious strudel. Care to join me?"

❦

Beck tried to draw out Houdini concerning the drama they had observed, but the magician had retreated into one of his pensive, thoughtful moods. Beck quickly gave up and the two men sat in companionable silence. Beck decided to work on a crossword, but soon made an irksome discovery. "Have you seen my new pen?" he asked Houdini.

"The Montblanc?" Houdini said.

"Yes! I left it right here!"

"Don't worry. I'm sure it will turn up."

"I hope so. Confound it, that thing was expensive." After a moment, he gave up and resorted to a pencil.

After a while, they were joined by Lachance, who entered carrying a bottle of brandy. "That man is impossible," Lachance grumbled as he sat down beside Houdini.

"What do you mean?" Beck asked.

"He patently refuses to admit this whole thing is a charade!"

"Perhaps it isn't," Houdini said.

"*Et tu*, Houdini?" Lachance said, pouring himself a generous portion of brandy. "Maybe I'll get lucky and he'll name *himself* as the killer. That would be nice." He laughed a little at his own joke, then fell silent as he sipped his drink.

Most of the other passengers had long since drifted back to their compartments, and the men were almost alone in the dining car. Almost.

Beck glanced up from his puzzle and met the stare of a small man with slicked-back hair and a pronounced overbite. The man quickly looked away, then furtively turned back, his large, wet eyes glistening as if he were some sort of amphibian. To Beck's dismay, the man stood up and made his way toward the table.

Houdini heard the man's approach. He turned and said: "Can I help you?"

The man gave an obsequious nod and dabbed at his brow with a handkerchief. "Well, yes, actually, I was wondering if...Oh, where are my manners..."

The man extended a hand and Houdini shook it.

"My name is Rudi Seiler," the man said. "It's a pleasure to meet you, sir, a real honor."

"What can I do for you, Herr Seiler?"

"I would like...I would like for you to stop Herr Ulrich's demonstration."

Lachance raised his glass. "A man after my own heart," he said.

"Why should I do that?" Houdini asked Seiler.

"Because it's a blasphemous fraud!" Seiler said with sudden vehemence. Beck and Lachance flinched at the outburst, but Houdini remained impassive.

"You're opposed to it on religious grounds?" the magician asked.

"On any grounds," Seiler said, regaining his composure. "I am surprised that you would condone this nonsense, considering your reputation…"

"I hope I have a reputation for being fair and open-minded," Houdini said.

"Yes, of course," Seiler said, looking embarrassed. "I'm just thinking of the other passengers, of the needless heartache that's been inflicted on the bereaved."

"That's very generous of you," Houdini said. "I'm sure they appreciate your sympathy."

Seiler's frog eyes narrowed. "Are you making fun of me?"

"I am not," Houdini said. "I am, however, curious as to why you feel so strongly about this."

Again, Seiler wiped his brow. He was sweating profusely. He spoke in a tremulous voice. "I take my morals very seriously, Herr Houdini."

"As do I," Houdini replied.

"See here, my good man," Lachance said. "Your objections have been duly noted. Now, can you not leave us in peace?"

Seiler gave a frustrated little harumph and stomped out of the car.

"Self-righteous prig," Lachance mumbled. "I'm sure he'll be sending at least a dozen letters of complaint to the board."

"Which they will surely disregard," Beck said.

"One can only hope," Lachance said.

On that note, the conversation ended, and the men retreated into their own thoughts.

Thirty minutes later, the conductor stepped into the car and informed them that Hans Ulrich was dead.

~つᴐᴑᴑᴇ~

"Murdered?" Lachance exclaimed. "How can you be sure of that?"

"There is a steak knife sticking out of the man's chest," said Albert Kalb. He had followed the conductor into the car and was standing behind him. "I found him that way just a few minutes ago. I informed Monsieur Roche, here, and he immediately brought me to you."

Beck spoke up: "Why didn't you go to the Berlin policeman, what was his name again?"

"Captain Nagel," Houdini said.

"It isn't my place," Roche said. "Monsieur Lachance is the most senior man on board the train…"

Beck looked at Lachance. The Belgian looked as if he'd like to jump out of the window. "My career is over," he muttered.

"Your career?" Kalb said. "Do you realize the position I'm in? The questions I'm going to be subjected to? My entire life is about to be turned inside-out!"

Houdini said: "I would like to see the body."

"Why?" Lachance demanded.

"Why not?" Houdini replied.

Lachance frowned. "We'll inform Nagel of what's happened," he said. "If he has no objections, then I suppose it's all right."

"Thank you," Houdini said.

Beck turned to his friend. "Listen, Harry," he said in an urgent whisper, "I don't want you sticking your nose into a murder investigation. The less we're involved in this, the better."

Houdini met Beck's level gaze. "Do you trust me?" he asked.

The odd question caught Beck by surprise. "Of course I do. You know that."

"Then follow my lead, and please don't argue."

～◌◌◌～

Ulrich stared up at the ceiling of his compartment, his waxen features fixed in a permanent mask of surprise. Beck, Houdini, and Nagel stood over the corpse, while Lachance, Kalb, and Roche crowded behind them in the open door.

"Hmm," Nagel said. He knelt down and inspected the knife. He lifted a hand as if to touch the handle, then seemed to change his mind. "Hmm," he said again.

"Any preliminary conclusions?" Houdini asked.

Nagel looked up, and for a moment Beck could have sworn that the man was utterly terrified. It was there in his eyes; a lightning strike of undisguised panic. It instantly disappeared, if it had truly been there at all, and Nagel regarded Houdini with cool disdain. "I prefer to keep my own counsel, thank you very much," he said.

Houdini did not reply, but Beck thought he saw a hint of wry amusement in the magician's eyes.

"So," Nagel said, rising to his considerable height. "Who was the last person to see this man alive?"

"Me, to the best of my knowledge," Lachance said.

"How long ago was that?"

"I'm not sure. Ninety minutes, perhaps."

"Were you with him in this compartment?"

"Yes, for about five or ten minutes. He locked the door behind me when I left."

"Why were you here?"

"I wanted him to tell me truth about his performance. I wanted to know if he was really going to accuse someone of murder."

"Did he say that he was?"

"Yes! I tried to get him to admit that the whole thing was a trick, but he was completely intractable."

"Why did you want him to make this admission?"

"So I could be assured that my company wasn't going to be involved in a lawsuit for slander!"

"Oh, come now," Nagel said. "Could you really be held accountable for the antics of a performer?"

"Perhaps not," Lachance conceded, "but the publicity would probably get me sacked."

"Ah, so you had motive to kill him?"

"I most certainly did not!" Lachance roared. "How dare you accuse me of this crime! Do you seriously think I would risk the guillotine over this arrogant popinjay? By God, I should sue *you* for slander!"

To Beck's surprise, Nagel shrank from this outburst. He stepped back and raised his hands, as if to ward off a physical attack. He actually looked as if he were about to offer an apology, but he was saved from this abasement by the intervention of Houdini.

"You shouldn't take this personally," the magician said to Lachance. "Asking offensive questions is just part of the Captain's job." Houdini turned to Nagel. "Isn't that right, Captain?"

"Yes," Nagel said quickly. "That's absolutely correct. Thank you, Herr Houdini."

Houdini held Nagel's eyes. "I'm sure the Inspector is going to want to interview everyone who was present at Ulrich's demonstration earlier this evening," he said. "I will volunteer to go first. Mr. Beck will join me so that we can be questioned together. You find this acceptable, don't you, Captain?"

"Yes, of course."

"Excellent. I think the dining car would be a good place to conduct the interviews. Wouldn't you agree?"

"Completely," said Nagel.

Beck could hardly believe his eyes. What was going on here? Had Houdini hypnotized the man?

"Wait just a minute," Kalb said. "Shouldn't we stop the train at the next station and alert the proper authorities?"

"That might give the killer an opportunity to slip away," Houdini said. "I think we should continue to Berlin. In fact, I'm willing to bet Captain Nagel will have the case solved well before we arrive."

"I appreciate the vote of confidence," Nagel said stiffly.

They all turned to Lachance. "Very well," he said at length. "The train will stay in motion. You may have the use of the dining car."

Beck wasn't sure if Lachance was speaking to Nagel or Houdini.

Beck and Houdini were back at their table in the dining car, facing a sour-faced Nagel over a pitcher of ice water.

"So," Houdini said, "what would you like to ask us first?"

Nagel thought about it for a moment. "Where were you between nine and ten?" he finally asked.

"We were both sitting right here," Houdini said.

"The entire time?"

"We never left the car."

Nagel sighed. He turned and looked out the window.

"May I ask a question?" Houdini said.

"Go ahead."

"How much was Ulrich paying you?"

Nagel closed his eyes. "A reasonable sum," he murmured.

"Paying him?" Beck said. "Paying him for what?"

Nagel gave Beck a sickly little half-smile. "I'm not a real policeman," he said. "I'm just an actor."

"Well, that's just great," Beck said. He turned to Houdini. "When did you tumble to this?"

"Almost immediately."

Nagel cleared his throat. "May I ask what gave me away?"

"It was nothing you did," Houdini said. "In fact, your performance was quite good."

"Then how on Earth...?"

"The success of Ulrich's demonstration hinged on him being able to unmask a murderer at midnight. If we reject the possibility that he was a bona-fide medium, we are confronted with two possibilities. Either he knew the identity of a genuine killer, and was concealing it for dramatic purposes, or..."

"Or he was going to supply his own," Beck said.

"Precisely," Houdini said. "And if that were the case, it naturally follows that he would supply his own policeman to arrest the malefactor."

Beck looked at Nagel. "Okay, if you're the fake cop, who's the fake killer?"

Nagel shrugged. "I have no idea. Ulrich told me to just follow his lead."

"That has a familiar ring," Beck said. "Why didn't you just admit all of this when you found out the old man was dead?"

"I was in shock," Nagel said. "Frankly, I wasn't even convinced he had actually been murdered until I saw the corpse. I thought it might have been another of his tricks, a ruse within a ruse!"

"Not the case, I'm afraid," Houdini said.

"So I discovered," Nagel said. "When I saw him there on the floor, I almost revealed everything, but then I became frightened that I would be in trouble. Impersonating a policeman is a serious crime, and I no longer had Herr Ulrich to explain things and accept responsibility."

Beck shook his head. "It took a hell of a nerve for you to imply that Lachance might have done it."

"That was very foolish of me. I was trying to brazen it out, for some stupid reason, at least until I had a chance to think things through. But then Herr Houdini stepped in..."

"Yeah," Beck said, "he stepped in it, all right."

Houdini smiled.

"So, now what do we do?" Beck demanded.

"We're going to solve this murder," Houdini said.

"You can't be serious."

Houdini's smile faded, and his eyes seemed to burn as they stared into Beck's. "Martin," he said, "that man was on this train because of me. He staged this entire thing for my benefit. And now he's dead."

"But you can't possibly hold yourself accountable."

"I don't," Houdini said. "I hold the killer accountable."

Beck was exasperated. "This is insane! We're not detectives! How can you possibly hope to identify the murderer before we pull into Berlin?"

Houdini turned up a palm. "By conducting a thorough investigation," he said.

~♧~

They began by interviewing Roche, the conductor. Nagel escorted him into the dining car and invited him to sit beside Beck.

"Why are these men still here?" Roche asked, indicating Beck and Houdini.

"They will be assisting me in my inquiries," Nagel said.

"Why?"

Nagel had been coached for this. "I have cleared them of all suspicion and recruited them to observe and take notes. It is possible that Herr Houdini may have some questions for you. If so, please respond to him just as you would me."

Roche appeared to consider a protest, but then he shrugged and sat down. Beck, who had been chosen for the role of secretary, lifted a pencil and prepared to transcribe the interview.

"When was the last time you saw Hans Ulrich alive?" Nagel asked. He was now firmly in character, and Beck believed the man was even enjoying himself a little.

"Here in the dining car."

"Did you speak to him at all after his demonstration?"

"I did not. I followed him and Monsieur Lachance back to Herr Ulrich's compartment. They stepped inside and closed the door behind them. I could hear them arguing."

"Did you hear anything specific?"

"No, nor did I attempt to. I can only imagine what would happen if Monsieur Lachance had opened the door and caught me eavesdropping."

"How long was he in there?"

"No more than ten minutes. When he emerged he slammed the door behind him. Then, he seemed to think of something else he wanted to say. He went back and tried the door, but it was locked. He demanded to be admitted, but Herr Ulrich ignored him. After a moment or two, he gave up. He turned to me and said he needed a drink, and asked if I would like to join him."

"Did you?"

"Yes. I followed him to the kitchen and made myself a sandwich. This was actually part of my normal routine. I always take my meals after the dinner service."

"How long were you there?"

"About a quarter of an hour. Monsieur Lachance took a bottle with him to the dining car, and I returned to my station in the sleeping car."

"Is that the only time you weren't at your station?"

"Yes."

"Did you see anyone else enter Ulrich's compartment before Herr Kalb discovered the body?"

"No."

"Ah-ha," Nagel said. "We have narrowed down the time of death. Ulrich was killed between nine-fifteen and nine-thirty. Make a note, Beck."

Beck gritted his teeth and made a note.

"Tell me, Roche," Houdini said, "do you have a passkey to the compartments?"

"I do."

"Does anyone else?"

"Not to my knowledge." Roche suddenly became alarmed. "Wait, are you implying…"

"I imply nothing," Houdini said. "We're simply gathering facts."

"Could anyone have taken the key from you?" Nagel asked.

Roche reached into a pocket and produced a key-ring. He singled out a key and held it up. "It's right here," he said.

"I see," Nagel said, "but a skilled pickpocket could have taken it and then returned it without you even knowing."

"Really?" Roche said. He brightened a little at this, as it seemed to divert suspicion from himself. "I suppose it's possible that someone could have lifted the keys…"

"It's also possible," Beck said, "that Ulrich could have just let someone in."

Roche liked this even more. "That's true!" he said. "The door wasn't locked when Herr Kalb found the body."

"Tell us about that," Houdini said.

"I was at my station when I saw Herr Kalb step out of his compartment and approach Herr Ulrich's door. He pounded on it for a moment, then tried the latch. I was about to tell him he shouldn't do that, when the door opened and Herr Kalb cried out in surprise."

"Kalb didn't actually enter the compartment?" Nagel asked.

"Not until I joined him. I immediately insisted that he come with me to find Monsieur Lachance. You know the rest."

"Indeed we do," Houdini said.

⁓꩜⁓

"I think he did it," Nagel said after Roche was gone.

"Really?" Houdini said.

"Tell me, Roche, do you have a passkey to the compartments?"

"Think about it! He has the key to the compartment. He enters after returning from the kitchen, stabs Ulrich, then leaves the door unlocked to divert suspicion from himself."

Houdini considered it. "And after killing Ulrich in cold blood, he waits in the sleeper for someone to discover the body?"

Nagel nodded. "He's a cool hand, this Roche."

"And his motive?" Beck asked.

Nagel waved at the question as if it were a mosquito. "Who knows? Maybe he actually killed someone in the past, and he feared Ulrich was going to name him at midnight."

"An interesting thought," Houdini said.

Nagel was excited. "Should we go ahead and denounce him?"

"Let's talk to some of the others first," Houdini said. "You know, just as a matter of form."

"Yes, of course," Nagel said. "Let's do."

⌁ↄ‿

"I did not kill that fraud!" Kalb bellowed. "And any man who claims I did will have to face me on the field of honor!"

"I'm sure it won't come to that," Houdini said in a mild tone.

"Well, what do you want from me? Go ahead and ask your questions!"

Nagel said: "Where were you between nine and ten?"

"I was in my compartment, stewing."

"Why did you go to Herr Ulrich's door?"

"I wanted him to tell me how he knew about my wife."

"Why did you try the door when he wouldn't answer?"

"Because I was furious! I still am!"

"Really?" Beck said. "I couldn't tell."

Kalb ignored him. "Theresa was the light of my life," he said. "For her to be reduced to a prop in a parlor trick..."

"Herr Kalb," Houdini said, "where is your compartment in relation to Ulrich's?"

"Right beside it."

"When you were stewing, as you say, did you hear anything from Ulrich's compartment? Any raised voices, perhaps?"

"I never heard anything except the noises of the train."

Nagel spoke up. "Did it ever occur to you, even for a moment, that Ulrich might really have been in contact with the spirit world?"

Kalb leaned forward and spoke in low growl. "If my wife's ghost wanted to communicate with me," he said, "she would have spoken directly to *me*, not through some third-rate conjurer."

Houdini cleared his throat. "Tell me, do you have any idea how Ulrich knew the details of your wife's death?"

"None whatsoever!"

"You haven't been discussing it with anyone recently? Perhaps in a situation where Ulrich could have overheard the conversation?"

Kalb's anger seemed to dissipate as he considered the question. "There was a time..." he said, then he shook his head. "No, no, it's quite impossible. He was nowhere near us."

"Us?" Houdini said.

"No, sir," Kalb said. "You'll not get another word out of me on that subject."

"Why not?"

"Because it can't possibly have anything to do with the man's death."

Nagel chose that moment to assert himself. "Perhaps you should let us be the judges of that."

Kalb turned on him. "And perhaps this crime should be investigated by an officer who doesn't need help from a magician!"

Nagel was stuck for an adequate response, so he settled for a stern glower. "You're free to go," he said.

～თ©～

"I've changed my mind," Nagel said. "*He* did it."

"You think so?" Houdini said.

"Not really," Nagel said, "but I'd like for it to be true."

Beck grunted. "You're shaping up to be one hell of a detective," he said.

"Well, I was an excellent Sergeant Cuff," Nagel replied.

"Who?"

Houdini chuckled. "It seems our friend, here, was in a production of *The Moonstone*." He looked at Nagel. "Is that how you got this job?"

"Herr Ulrich was very impressed," Nagel said.

Beck decided to get back down to cases. "Who's next?" he asked.

～თ©～

"I would appreciate if you would excuse my wife from this inquiry," said Michel Cloutier.

"Please, Michel," his wife said softly. "I can speak for myself."

"Of course," Cloutier said, "but surely these man can't possibly think..."

"Michel," she said, "it's a murder investigation. No one is above suspicion."

Cloutier turned to Nagel, as if seeking confirmation of this statement.

"Personally," Nagel said, "I don't think it likely that…"

"Perhaps it would be best," Houdini interrupted, "if we spoke to Monsieur Cloutier alone."

Cloutier gave Houdini a narrow-eyed stare, then slowly nodded. "Will you excuse us, my dear?"

The woman hesitated, then gave her husband a weak smile. "I'll be waiting in our compartment."

After she was gone, Cloutier turned a steely gaze on Nagel. "Who is in charge, here? You or this man?" He pointed at Houdini.

Nagel gave him same little speech he had given Roche.

Cloutier wasn't impressed. "Speak to him as I would you? I don't think so. You'll forgive me if I'm not enamored of magicians right now."

Nagel, to his credit, took this in stride. "As you wish," he said. "Tell me, when did you last see Herr Ulrich alive?"

"The same time you did, presumably."

"At the end of his performance, you mean?"

"Yes."

"It seemed to me that you were very angry with him."

"Why wouldn't I be? You saw the state my wife was in."

"Do you think it's possible that Herr Ulrich received a message from…"

"Stop right there," Cloutier said. "I do not wish to discuss that."

"Sir," Nagel said, "as your wife correctly pointed out, this is a murder investigation. You are in no position to dictate terms to me about what I may or may not ask. Do I make myself clear?"

Cloutier sighed. "Damnation," he muttered. "Very well, ask whatever you like."

Nagel gave Beck a quick glance, as if to say, *See, told you I was good.* "As I was saying," he continued, "do you believe that Herr Ulrich could have received a message from your son?"

"Yes," Cloutier said.

Nagel couldn't hide his surprise. "You do?"

"I think it's possible. Not likely, but possible."

"Then why were you so hostile to Herr Ulrich?"

"I was afraid he might be lying, that he was simply using us as part of his act."

"Indeed. You told him that he would regret it if that were the case."

"Did I say that?"

"I heard you. So did many others"

"Well, I didn't kill him, if that's what you're saying. In fact, I grieve for the man, more than you can imagine."

"Really?"

"Of course! Now we'll never know if he really spoke to Henri! We were daring to hope that once...just this *once*..." Cloutier took a deep breath and slowly exhaled. "You have no idea how horrible it's been for us. We have tried to contact our son many times, through many different mediums, all to no avail. They have invariably turned out to be charlatans."

Nagel shook his head. "I don't understand you at all. If that's been your experience, then why would you believe Ulrich might be genuine?"

"Because I *want* to believe," Cloutier said, and for the first time Beck could see the true depths of the man's pain. "I want to believe that we can hear from him again, that we can hear his voice, see his face, know that he's happy...I...want...to believe..."

Cloutier was trembling. He covered his eyes, making a visible effort to control himself. Nagel cast an inquiring glance at Houdini, and the magician nodded.

"I think we're finished for now, Monsieur Cloutier," Nagel said.

Cloutier left without saying a word.

⌁∞⌁

"Well, I think it's safe to cross him off," Nagel said.

"I'm not so sure," Beck said. "What if he somehow figured out that Ulrich was a fake?"

"Hmm," Nagel said, "I see what you mean. One more liar playing games with his pain. The disappointment could have easily turned to rage."

Houdini drummed the table with the fingers of his left hand. "But how could he have figured it out?" he asked.

Nagel rose to the challenge. "He went to Ulrich's compartment, and forced him to tell the truth. When Ulrich admitted that he was a fraud, Cloutier lost control and killed him."

"Cloutier," Beck said, "or his wife."

Nagel shook his head. "Oh, now *that* I don't accept."

"Why not?" Beck asked. "Do you believe women are incapable of murder?"

"I didn't say that. Don't put words in my mouth."

Houdini leaned forward. "If we accept Roche's story," he said, "then there is only a fifteen minute window for the crime. In that span of time, one or both of the Cloutiers would have had to talk Ulrich into letting them in, pressured him into admitting his deception, killed him, and then slipped away unobserved…" Houdini's brow knitted as considered this possibility.

"That scenario applies to all the suspects," Beck said. "It's just as likely, or *unlikely*, for the others as it is for the Cloutiers."

"It's a lot to happen in a quarter of an hour," Houdini said. "Especially without enough noise being made to draw Kalb's attention in the compartment next door."

"If Kalb is telling the truth," Nagel said. His eyes lit up and he snapped his fingers. "Perhaps Kalb *did* hear something. What if he heard Monsieur Cloutier confront and kill Ulrich? He could have opened his door in time to see Cloutier emerge red-handed, so to speak."

Beck couldn't see it. "Then why didn't Kalb raise the alarm?"

Nagel was ready for that. "Kalb despised Ulrich, so he might have agreed to cover for Cloutier, perhaps demanding a bribe for added incentive."

"All within fifteen minutes," Houdini said.

"It's not impossible," Nagel said.

"No," Houdini conceded. "It's not impossible. Not quite."

Beck rubbed his eyes. His head was starting to hurt. "Who's next?" he asked

"I think it's time we tied up a loose end," Houdini said.

~ঞ৹৴

"Herr Seiler," said Nagel, "could you please tell us where you were between nine and ten?"

"I was in this car until quarter 'til ten," Seiler said, mopping his brow. "These men can vouch for me."

"And after that?"

"I returned to my compartment, where I remained until I was summoned for this interview."

Nagel looked at Houdini. It was clear that he wasn't sure where to go next. If Roche's timetable was accurate, then Seiler had been in full view of Houdini and Beck when the crime took place. He could be ruled out as a suspect, so why were they even talking to him?

Houdini steepled his fingers beneath his chin. "Is there anything you would like to tell us, Herr Seiler? Anything at all that might help to expedite this inquiry?"

Seiler's tongue passed over his protruding incisors. "No," he said.

Houdini slowly shook his head. "You disappoint me, sir." He turned to Nagel. "Captain, this man is a murderer."

Beck wasn't sure who was more surprised, Nagel or Seiler. They gawked at Houdini, then at each other.

"Wait!" Seiler cried. "This is a mistake! I haven't hurt anyone! I'm just... I'm just..."

It was at that moment that Beck saw the truth. "You're just an actor," he said.

Seiler looked at Beck as a drowning man might look upon a lifeboat. "Yes!" he said. "I was hired by Herr Ulrich to play the role of a killer in his performance. He was going to 'unmask' me at midnight!"

"You jackass!" Beck said. "Why didn't you tell us that up front?"

"I wanted to avoid being caught up in a murder investigation. I knew I had an ironclad alibi because of the time I spent in the dining car. I hoped that if I kept a low profile, I could just disappear after we got to Berlin."

Beck wanted to punch the man. "Fat chance of that," he said.

"Mr. Beck is right," Houdini told Seiler. "You have been very foolish, my friend, but I'm grateful for your mistake."

"Why is that?" Seiler asked.

"By remaining silent, you have allowed us to maintain Captain Nagel's imposture. Without that, we wouldn't have been able to pursue this matter."

"Lucky us," Beck said.

Seiler turned to Nagel. "So you *are* a fake! I figured you had to be, but I wasn't completely sure."

Nagel took this as a compliment. "I am very believable, if I say so myself."

Beck wanted to punch him, too.

Seiler looked at Houdini. "How did you know I was an actor?"

"Are you familiar with 'Occam's razor'?" Houdini asked.

"I'm afraid not."

"Well, to put it in somewhat reductive terms, it's a principle that states the simplest solution is usually the correct one. Of all the passengers who attended Ulrich's performance, you were the one who most fit the bill as the pseudo-murderer."

"Then you weren't really sure just now? You were just guessing?"

"A guess informed by many years of experience in the art of illusion. Also, I have to say that you slightly overplayed your hand. That little scene you performed here in the dining car..."

Seiler winced. "Too much?"

Houdini nodded. "And then there's those teeth."

Seiler reached up and plucked the front teeth from his mouth, revealing a pair of perfectly normal incisors beneath. "I thought they were good enough to fool anyone," he said.

"I'm not just anyone," Houdini said.

～ｏℚℴ～

They sent Seiler back to his compartment and told him to wait there until he was told otherwise.

"Well," Beck said, "we've unveiled a bogus killer, but I don't think we're any closer to catching a real one."

"Don't be discouraged," Houdini said. "We know a lot more than we did a few hours ago, and there are still some important people to interview."

"There are? Who?"

～ｏℚℴ～

"You can't possibly think that I or my granddaughter had anything to do with this crime," announced Claudette Debans. Her neck wattles were shaking with fury, and Beck forced himself not to stare at them. He looked at the young girl, and her embarrassment was clearly written on her features. Red-faced and frowning, she studied the floor as if the answers to all of life's mysteries could be found there. Beck felt sorry for her.

"Of course not," Nagel said, following the script Houdini had given him. "There are just some routine questions I have to ask. I promise it won't take more than a few minutes."

"Ask, then!"

"Ah, Madame, there are some details of the crime which are not fit for the ears of a young girl. Unfortunately, we will be required to discuss them. If I could prevail upon you to join me in private…"

"What, and leave Sylvie alone with these two?" She looked and Beck and Houdini as if they were a pair of drooling madmen.

"Please, Madame, it would be better for all concerned if you would comply."

"I don't think…"

"I insist," Nagel said, a bit of steel gleaming in his voice.

Madame Debans relented, giving Nagel an angry little nod and allowing him to lead her away. Beck watched them exit the car, and grudgingly admitted to himself that Nagel had played his part to perfection.

Houdini gently took the girl's arm and ushered her to a seat. "Please sit down," he said. "Would you like a glass of water?"

The girl shook her head.

"I am Harry Houdini, and this is my friend, Martin Beck. Your name is Sylvie, is that correct?"

The girl nodded.

"Sylvie," Houdini said, "you seem like a very bright girl, and I have a feeling you can help us with this investigation."

For the first time, the girl met Houdini's eyes. "I can? How?"

"During Herr Ulrich's performance, he said that there was a thief in the room..." Houdini let the sentence hang.

Sylvie's face reddened. "I remember," she said.

"Do you have any idea who he was referring to?"

"No, Monsieur, I do not."

"I think you do."

"Are you accusing me?"

"I am," Houdini said with a friendly smile.

Beck expected the girl to follow her grandmother's fulminating example, but instead she went perfectly still. She didn't even seem to be breathing. Beck had the feeling that if he reached out and tapped her, she would crack and fall apart. Then she rallied and forced herself to respond. "And do you have proof?" she asked.

Houdini flicked his wrist, and Beck's missing Montblanc appeared in his hand. Beck's surprise at this sleight of hand was compounded when he saw Sylvie unconsciously reach for one the pockets of her coat.

Houdini was still smiling. "I took it from you when I was helping you to your seat."

Sylvie turned to Beck, tears streaming from her eyes. "I'm so sorry, Monsieur! Please forgive me! Please! I cannot help myself! I have a disease...a compulsion..."

Beck was embarrassed. "Stop that," he said, producing a handkerchief and passing it to the girl. "I have the pen back and no more need be said about it."

Houdini shook his head. "I'm afraid a little more does need to be said."

Sylvie, now sobbing uncontrollably, buried her face in Beck's handkerchief. "Please don't tell *mémé*. She will be so angry, so ashamed. Oh, I beg of you..."

"Look at me," Houdini said.

Sylvie lowered the handkerchief. Her red-rimmed eyes focused on the magician.

"Your secret is safe with us," Houdini said. "I just need you to answer a few questions, completely and honestly. Will you do that?"

Sylvie nodded vigorously.

"All right," Houdini said. "I saw you palm Mr. Beck's pen while everyone was distracted in the aftermath of Ulrich's performance..."

"Wait a minute," Beck interrupted. "You mean you knew all along that..."

Houdini silenced him with a gesture. "It was a reasonable surmise that you were the thief Ulrich had referred to earlier, but how did he know about you? Do you have any idea? Is there anything he might have seen you take?"

"No one saw..." Sylvie began, and then she choked and started to weep again. She pressed her lips together and took a moment to recover herself. "This is very difficult for me," she said. "It is very hard for to me to talk about what I have done."

"We're not here to judge you," Houdini said. "Please continue."

"I stole...I stole the blind woman's change purse."

"Fräulein Richter," Houdini said. "She mentioned that it was missing."

"I was returning from the lavatory when I noticed it on the seat beside her. She was alone, and no one was watching..."

"How could you be sure?"

"I have been doing this since I was a small child. I am very good at it. I always know when people are not paying attention."

"Not always," Houdini pointed out.

"You are different," Sylvie said, and Beck heard a note of admiration in her voice.

"Perhaps Ulrich was different, too. How do you know he wasn't watching?"

"He was facing the opposite direction. Unless he had eyes in the back of his head..."

"Or supernatural powers," Houdini said.

Sylvie blanched. "I think he really did talk to spirits," she whispered. "When he said there was a thief on the train, and that he knew who it was, I was terrified. I had promised *mémé* I would never steal again, but I just can't seem to..."

Houdini held up a hand. "Please," he said, "tell us what you did after the demonstration. Did you attempt to return the purse, as Ulrich commanded."

"Yes."

"It is very hard for to me to talk about what I have done."

"Did you admit to Fräulein Richter what you had done?"

The girl looked away. She bit her lower lip.

"Sylvie?"

"I did not speak to Fräulein Richter. I went to the compartment of Herr Ulrich. I was going to give him the purse and ask him to return it for me. I wanted to apologize, and beg him not to tell…"

Houdini leaned forward. "Did you talk to him?"

Sylvie took a deep breath and slowly exhaled. "I was watching through a crack in my door when Monsieur Lachance left Herr Ulrich's compartment. I wanted to go to him then, but I didn't have the nerve. I sat down on my bunk, and took a few minutes to work up my courage. Then I went to his door, but he didn't answer my knock. I tried the latch, and found that it was unlocked. I opened it…"

"And you saw his body," Houdini said.

Sylvie nodded. "I closed the door returned to my own compartment. I didn't tell anyone what I had seen. I was so frightened…"

Beck could no longer maintain his silence. "Did you see anyone else? Anyone at all?"

"No."

"What about the conductor?"

"He was not in the car."

"Do you know what time this was?"

"I cannot be sure, Monsieur. I do not carry a watch. All I can tell you is that it was five or six minutes after Monsieur Lachance and the conductor left the car."

"Sylvie," Houdini said, "I believe we're done for now. You can rejoin your grandmother. I have a feeling Captain Nagel will be finished with her soon after he sees you."

Sylvie stood up and turned to go, then paused and looked at Houdini. "Are you going to tell anyone…?"

"About your petty thievery?" Houdini asked.

Sylvie winced, as if the words physically stung. "Yes."

"I have given you my word," Houdini said. "I have never broken it before, and I don't intend to start now. Do you still have Fräulein Richter's property?"

Sylvie reached into her coat and retrieved a small change purse. She passed it to Houdini.

"I will return this for you," Houdini said, "and I strongly advise you not to do anything like this again."

"I have tried to stop, Monsieur. I just can't help myself."

"I'm no psychologist," Houdini said, "so I won't comment on that. I will say this: You have a deft hand and a knack for subtlety. Perhaps you should give magic a try."

Sylvie blinked in surprise. "Do you think I would be good at it?"

"You will never know unless you try."

Sylvie grinned. "Thank you, Monsieur."

"You're welcome, Sylvie."

⌘

"We've narrowed the window of opportunity to five or six minutes," Nagel said. "This is a major clue."

"Yes, but to what?" Beck said. "I don't see how it's brought us any closer to the truth. At least her story coincides with everything Lachance and Roche told us. That's something, isn't it?"

Beck and Nagel both turned to Houdini. The magician didn't seem to notice. His gaze was turned inward, focused on some vista that only he could see. "The simplest solution…" he murmured.

"Harry?" Beck said.

"I know who did it," Houdini said.

Beck and Nagel stared at him. After a moment, Beck said: "Well? Are you going to keep us in suspense all night?"

Houdini gave them a name, and an explanation. When he was finished, Nagel let out a low whistle. "Amazing," he said. "You've covered all the facts, but is there any real proof?"

"None, I'm afraid," Houdini said. "The case is highly circumstantial."

"Well, you've convinced me," Beck said. "Let's give it to the Berlin police. They can finish what we've started."

"I'd prefer to finish it myself," Houdini said.

"Really?" Beck said. "May I ask how?"

"By obtaining a confession."

Beck threw up his hands. "Of course!" he said. "It's so obvious! We just confront the killer with your theory, and let a guilty conscience do the rest!"

Houdini gave him a pat on the shoulder. "You get very irritable when you're tired, you know that?"

"Yes, actually, I do. Why don't you brighten my mood by telling me your brilliant plan."

"I will, but first there's one last person we need to talk to."

"I think I can guess who," Beck said.

⌘

It was after one o'clock in the morning, but none of the people in the dining car looked very sleepy. Beck surveyed their drawn features. It was the same group of individuals that had made up Ulrich's audience earlier. Now, they were here for a different kind of show.

"This is ridiculous," grumbled Albert Kalb. "Why have we been summoned here in the middle of the night? Haven't we been subjected to enough?" He looked around at his fellow passengers, but they ignored him. Their eyes were focused on the magician at the head of the car.

"Thank you all for coming," Houdini said to them. "I appreciate how tired you all must be, and how difficult the last few hours have been for you. However, if you will bear with me for a short time, I believe I can bring this wretched affair to a satisfactory conclusion."

"By exposing Ulrich's murderer?" Kalb scoffed.

"Precisely," Houdini said.

It was clear that Kalb hadn't really expected that. He didn't say anything else.

"A few hours ago," Houdini said, "standing in this very spot, Hans Ulrich claimed to make contact with the spirit world. He made some amazing revelations, the most startling of which was the presence of a murderer in the audience."

"Yes, yes, we remember," said Madame Debans, her neck wattles wobbling. "He said he would name them at midnight."

"Indeed, he did," Houdini said, "but someone decided to make sure that wouldn't happen. After the demonstration, Ulrich returned to his compartment, followed by Monsieur Lachance. There, they had a brief argument. Monsieur Lachance left Ulrich's room, but then turned back. He tried to open Ulrich's door, but it was locked. He knocked on the door, but Ulrich refused to admit him." Houdini looked at Lachance. "Is that correct, Monsieur?"

Lachance cleared his throat. "Yes," he said.

"May I ask what made you try to resume your conversation with Herr Ulrich?"

Lachance squirmed in his chair. "Do I have to do this here? In front of all these people?"

"Please."

"Oh, very well. I was going to offer him a bribe to call off his second demonstration. I just wanted the whole thing to stop before it became any more embarrassing."

Houdini nodded. "And then you invited Monsieur Roche to join you in the kitchen for a drink?"

"Yes."

Houdini turned to the conductor. "Roche, do you agree with this account of events?"

"Yes, Monsieur."

"And did you accept Lachance's invitation?"

"I did. I had a sandwich and returned to the sleeper after about fifteen minutes."

"And there you remained until Herr Kalb discovered Ulrich's body."

"Yes."

"Did you see anyone else enter the car or approach Herr Ulrich's room?"

Roche shook his head.

Houdini turned to Kalb. "Your compartment is next to Herr Ulrich's, is it not?"

"It is," Kalb said warily. "I went there after the performance and stayed there until I found the old goat's body."

"And did you see, or more importantly, *hear*, anything at all?"

"I did not," Kalb said.

"Then we are confronted with an interesting problem," Houdini said. "If everything we've heard thus far is true, it seems clear that someone talked their way into Ulrich's compartment, murdered him in complete silence, and then disappeared without a trace, all within a quarter of an hour."

"Hardly impossible," Kalb said.

"No," Houdini said, "but it's a narrow window of opportunity. Now, suppose I were to tell you that someone found Herr Ulrich dead at some point *during* those fifteen minutes. Someone innocent of the murder, but who nonetheless feared to step forward for other, personal reasons..."

Kalb stood up. "I would ask you to produce that person!"

"Calm yourself," Houdini said. His tone was mild, but it held a note of unmistakable command. "Think about what I am saying. If this person's word is good, and I believe it is, then what does that mean to the investigation?"

To everyone's surprise, it was Madame Cloutier who answered. "The time narrows even more," she said. "The killer must have the luck of the devil."

"You are correct," Houdini said. "It has been said that fortune favors the bold, and we are dealing with a murderer who is bold, decisive, and ruthless. But this killer's luck is about to run out."

Lachance spoke up. "Why do you say that? Is there some evidence that you've discovered?"

"Better than that," Houdini said. "We are going to hear from an eyewitness."

Houdini raised his hand, and the door behind him opened. Anna Richter stepped into the car, guided by the solicitous hand of Captain Nagel.

Kalb was on his feet again. "This is your witness? A blind woman?"

"Of course not," Houdini said.

"Well, who is it, then?"

"You met him earlier. He called himself Den."

"The ghost? He was a fabrication of that liar, Ulrich!"

"Was he?" Houdini asked. "I believe that you are incorrect. I believe that Den was very real, and that he spoke to us, and that he will speak to us again."

Everyone in the car gawked at the magician in stunned disbelief. Even Kalb was startled out of his anger.

Houdini stretched the moment for effect, then resumed. "It is true that I am well-known for my skepticism with regard to mediums, but Herr Ulrich forced me to re-examine my beliefs. I am convinced that he was completely genuine. I have studied his notes, and I think I can establish contact with the Egyptian spirit. It is my hope that Den will reveal to us the name of Ulrich's killer."

"But why is Fräulein Richter here?" Kalb asked.

"I am not as well versed in these matters as Ulrich was," Houdini said. "I require an assistant, and who better to see through the third eye than someone whose senses have been enhanced by the loss of their earthly vision?"

"I am only too glad to help," Anna Richter said with a weak smile.

Houdini made a small gesture, and Beck pulled up a chair behind the blind woman. Nagel helped her into the seat, and Houdini stepped into place behind her. He placed his hands on her shoulders, and looked out on the passengers. "I will require complete silence," he said.

Beck expected a challenge, from the recalcitrant Kalb, if no one else, but the passengers were mesmerized by the spectacle unfolding before them. Beck sought out a particular pair of eyes, and studied them for signs of hidden guilt. He was rewarded by the sight of a thin trickle of sweat running down the person's face.

"Anna Richter," Houdini said, "focus on my voice...my voice...only my voice..."

"Your voice..." the woman said.

"My hands are upon your shoulders. You feel as if they are gently lifting you…lifting you into the air…setting you free from the bonds of the earth…"

"I feel…I feel as if I'm floating…"

"Yes, you are floating…floating into the ether…and now you can see…"

"Yes! Yes! I can see! I can see light!"

Anna Richter began to thrash about as if she had been exposed to an electrical current. Houdini held her in place as she flailed, her clouded eyes rolling wildly. Then she became completely still. She slumped in the chair, and then lifted her head. Her face was set in an expression of scornful hauteur. "What is this?" she asked. "Why am I trapped in darkness?"

"The vessel you are inhabiting is blind," Houdini said. "May I ask to whom I am speaking."

"I am Den, son of Queen Merneith, King of the Two Lands. Is that you, soothsayer?"

"I am the showman, Houdini, and I am in need of your assistance."

"What would you have me do?"

"Your acquaintance, Hans Ulrich, has been murdered."

"I am aware of the fact. I can hear the cries of his spirit. He yearns to join us here on the other side, but he cannot move on until his killer is brought to justice."

"That is what we wish to do. Who killed Hans Ulrich?"

The woman tilted her head. "My gaze pierces the mists of time," she said. "I behold a moment scant hours ago. I watch as Ulrich exits a dining room filled with people. They stare after him in anger and hope and distrust…*and fear*…"

"There is someone who fears him?"

"Oh, yes. He is terrified of Ulrich. He thinks the old man has seen into the dark past, and that he will, with my help, expose a guilty secret that will destroy…destroy…destroy…"

She trailed into silence, then took a slow, deep breath.

"He follows Ulrich from the room, slipping a knife from a table as he passes by. He dogs Ulrich's heels to his compartment, demanding to speak to him alone…"

"No," Lachance whispered, and every eye in the car fell on him.

"Yes!" the woman said. "I know that voice. It is voice of the killer. He is arguing with Ulrich, insisting that he call off the second performance. Ulrich refuses. The killer produces the knife. He strikes!"

"Lies," Lachance gasped. He stood and made as if to storm up the aisle, but Nagel blocked his way.

"The killer leaves the compartment," Anna Richter said. "He steps into the hall and sees the conductor. He makes a production of going back to the door, rattling the latch, pretending it is locked..."

"Pretending?" Roche said. He stared at Lachance as if the man had suddenly sprouted horns.

"Lies!" Lachance shouted. "All lies!"

"You say that Den is a liar?" Houdini said, his voice low and dangerous.

"I say that all of you are liars and frauds! I wasn't afraid of Ulrich! He was a charlatan!"

"He communed with the spirits," Houdini said. "You silenced him before they could name you as a killer, but that will not stop them. They will have their justice."

"This is completely insane!" Lachance cried. He was on the verge of hysterics. He looked to his fellow passengers. "You people can't be taking any of this seriously! You can't!"

"You seem to be," Kalb said.

"I'm being accused of murder, you insufferable ass! How am I supposed to act?"

"I never actually checked the door," Roche murmured. "I just took your word for it..."

"Roche!" Lachance said. "Hold your tongue, damn you!"

Roche didn't hold his tongue. "Were you hoping they would suspect me?" he said. "That they would accuse me of the crime because I had the keys?"

"I wasn't hoping for anything because *I didn't do it!*"

"You did," Anna Richter said. "You did, and you will confess."

"Like hell, I will!"

"Hell is what you face, Claude Lachance," the blind woman said. "I know you believe in the power of the spirits, despite all your feeble protests. You knew that my servant, Ulrich, was going to expose you, and so you struck him down. But you cannot do the same for me. You cannot kill that which is already dead!"

Lachance went pale as alabaster. "I don't believe in you," he croaked.

Fräulein Richter smiled. "Confess your crime, or face a punishment far worse than any you can imagine."

"No!"

Houdini and the blind woman spoke together, their voices forming an eerie chorus. *"Still you claim to doubt?"* Houdini lifted his hands from Anna Richter's shoulders, and placed them over her eyes. *"Then behold this demonstration of my power!"*

Houdini pulled back his hands to reveal the eyes of Anna Richter. No longer clouded and gray, they were now clear, green, and glittering. They seemed to burn with a verdant fire as they gazed at Lachance.

"I see you," Fräulein Richter said, pointing at Lachance. "I see your guilt and your fear and your shame."

It was too much for Lachance. He fell to his knees in the aisle. "My God," he said. "Oh, my God…"

Fräulein Richter rose from her chair and walked to Lachance. She stood over him, her emerald eyes pitiless and implacable. "Confess," she whispered.

"I killed him," Lachance said, and then he began to weep.

～つℚC⌐

"Thank you for agreeing to meet with us," Michel Cloutier said as he held the chair for his wife.

"No need to thank us," Houdini said.

"Indeed," Beck said. "It's the least we could do."

After Madame Cloutier was seated, the men took their place at the table. They were at *Zur Lezten Instanz*, a Berlin restaurant distinguished by its age. It was said that Napoleon had dined there.

They ordered drinks, and then Cloutier said: "I will come directly to the point. It has been two days since our…eventful journey…and my wife and I have been unable to get satisfactory answers from anyone as to what exactly took place during that second demonstration."

"I gather the Berlin police have been less than forthcoming," Houdini said.

"To say the least. We very much wanted to speak with you that night, but after Lachance's public confession…"

"Yes," Houdini said, "it was something of a whirlwind, wasn't it?"

"It was," Cloutier said.

Madame Cloutier leaned forward. "Please," she said, "I simply must know. Did you really cure that woman's blindness?"

"I did not," Houdini said. "It was all an illusion."

It was obvious that she had expected this reply, but she still looked crestfallen. "Then you didn't make contact with the spirits?"

"If there were any spirits on that train," Houdini said, "they did not speak to me."

"Then what did we see?" Monsieur Cloutier asked.

"Allow me to start at the beginning," the magician said.

Houdini was succinct, but thorough. He told them how he had deduced the true identity of Captain Nagel, and why he decided to enlist the man's aid in conducting a private investigation. He briefly sketched out the details of their interviews, including his exposure of Seiler as a fraud. He confided that he had discovered the identity of a petty thief, but he did the mention the name of Sylvie Debans.

"When the thief admitted pilfering the blind woman's purse, that was when I became certain that Anna Richter was not what she appeared to be."

"Why do you say that?" asked Monsieur Cloutier.

"Ulrich had to have a third confederate. Nagel and Seiler were merely actors, but someone else had to be feeding him information about the other passengers. How else to explain his intimate knowledge of Kalb's misfortunes?"

"And our own." Cloutier said.

"Precisely."

"She had sat with us when we took the train from Cologne a week earlier…"

"That was a trial run, to test her imposture and establish her identity. It was serendipitous for her that you ended up on the express to Berlin. When she told Ulrich about your tragic circumstances, he couldn't resist incorporating it into his performance."

"The swine," Cloutier muttered.

"Try not to judge him too harshly," Houdini said. "I think he honestly believed he was doing more good than harm."

"By teasing us with false hopes?"

Houdini nodded. "I believe he realized he had made a mistake when he saw how much distress he was causing you and Herr Kalb, but by then it was too late. He was committed to his course of action, and he couldn't turn back."

"When exactly did you begin to suspect Fräulein Richter?"

"The biggest clue was Kalb's refusal to reveal who he had confided his troubles to. Why was he so reluctant to suspect this person, and why did he seem so protective of them? Kalb is an abrasive and tempestuous fellow. Who among our fellow passengers could inspire in him such warmth and trust? A friendly and sympathetic blind woman seemed the most likely candidate."

"That makes sense," Cloutier said.

"When the thief confessed to stealing Fräulein Richter's purse, they told me they were convinced no one had witnessed the deed. I was inclined to believe this, but if it were true, how did Ulrich know the thief's identity?"

"Of course!" Madame Cloutier said. "Fräulein Richter saw the theft herself!"

"Exactly," Houdini said. "She shared this information with Ulrich, and he used in his act."

"But her eyes," Madame Cloutier said, "how did she disguise them?"

"That was a brilliant touch," Houdini said. "She was wearing small glass lenses placed directly on her corneas. They were horribly uncomfortable, but they gave her every appearance of being completely blind without actually impeding her vision. At the appropriate moment, I gently removed them, thus achieving the desired effect."

"That woman should be brought up on charges," Cloutier said.

"She has committed no crime," Houdini said. "She was an actress hired to perform a role, which she did remarkably well. When I informed her than I had penetrated her ruse, and that I wanted her help in apprehending Ulrich's murderer, she happy to assist."

"What about Nagel?" Cloutier asked. "He impersonated a police officer. Will he be arrested?"

Houdini smiled. "I have persuaded the authorities that Nagel acted honorably in the interest of justice, and deserved to be treated accordingly."

Cloutier was impressed. "Do you really have so much influence with the *polizei*?"

Houdini shrugged. "Fame has its advantages."

"What of Monsieur Lachance?" Madame Cloutier asked. "Does anyone know why he killed Herr Ulrich?"

"It seems that Lachance was hiding a guilty secret," Houdini said. "Many years ago, he killed his mistress, and managed to escape suspicion. When Ulrich threatened to name a murderer, Lachance was seized with mortal terror, and he acted upon that fear."

"Then he really did believe in the power of the spirits?"

"I decided to take the risk that he did. Fortunately, my gamble paid off."

"Yes, but how did you know it was him?" Cloutier demanded.

"It was a logical inference," Houdini said. "The alternative was a killer of almost supernatural speed, stealth, and cunning."

"Like a spirit," Madame Cloutier said.

"And we know how Houdini feels about spirits," her husband added. He intended it as a witticism, but it fell flat, and there was a moment of awkward silence.

"Monsieur Houdini," Madame Cloutier said softly.

"Yes?"

"Do think there is any hope...any hope at all...that we will speak to Henri again?"

Beck watched Houdini from the corner of his eye. Prior to the meal, he and the magician had discussed the possibility that this question might arise, and how best to address it.

These people have had their hearts trampled, Beck had said. *I don't want to say anything that will add to their pain.*

Nor do I, Houdini had replied, *but I don't want to lie to them either.*

"Monsieur?" Madame Cloutier said.

Houdini leaned forward. "Madame Cloutier," he said, "I'm sorry, but I do not think you will hear from your son again in this life."

And there it was. The plain truth. But was it what the woman needed to hear?

Madame Cloutier looked at her husband, then back at Houdini. She reached out and took the magician's hand. "In that case," she said, "I will live this life to the fullest, and hope for the best in the next."

Houdini smiled. "That is a simple solution," he said, "but the simplest solutions are usually the correct ones."

The End

NOTES ON "MAGICIAN'S RAZOR"

This story is my first attempt at a "whodunit" in the Agatha Christie tradition. It obviously owes a great deal to Dame Agatha's great classics "Mystery of the Blue Train" and Murder on the Orient Express," but I was equally influenced by Rex Stout's "Nero Wolfe" series, of which I am a huge fan.

Although I have always loved mysteries, the experience of working on this project gave me a renewed appreciation for the talents and skills of the writers who specialize in this genre. *Am I giving away too much? Too little? Is my detective too clever to be believable? Or am I making him act embarrassingly dumb?* Questions like these plagued me the whole way through the process. How well I responded to these difficulties remains for the reader to decide.

Although the Harry Houdini depicted here is a fictional creation, I drew a great deal of inspiration from the real man's life. One of the most interesting resources I used was *The Secret Life of Harry Houdini: The Making of America's First Superhero* by William Kalush and Larry Sloman. It's an eccentric book with many detractors, but I found it to be immensely readable, and I would recommend it to anyone wanting to learn more about the Master Mystifier.

I would like to publicly thank Ron Fortier for inviting me aboard this particular train, and to express my appreciation to my fellow authors Jim Beard, James Palmer, and Ian Watson for their patience and encouragement. It's been a privilege, guys.

ROMAN LEARY - was eight years old when a family friend gave him an Ace paperback of Conan stories. He has been a devotee of pulp fiction ever since. Today, he lives in North Carolina with his wife and their beautiful daughter. His first novel, *Brother Bones: Six Days of the Dragon*, was recently published by Airship 27.

HOLMES & HOUDINI

BY I.A. WATSON

"Oh, Harry has his own ideas about what he wants to do. The ideal client would turn up at his performances, sober and punctual, do his act, take a bow, talk to the press, and retire quietly till it's time to get on the train to the next venue. That's all we agents ask, really."

"Houdini is not sober and prompt?"

"Oh, that's not my problem, Dr Watson. I could handle an unprofessional drunk. I have done. But a guy who insists on chasing down frauds and hucksters, who'll never turn his back on a gal in distress or a puzzle that can't be solved? It makes for an exciting tour, you know?"

I couldn't restrain a sigh of sympathy. "There are some men who are fated for such extraordinary adventures, I'm afraid."

"And some who have to put up with 'em," Beck replied. "Come to the opening if you can. Houdini's a big admirer of Sherlock Holmes. He'd like to meet him."

"Holmes is shy of publicity," I warned. "I doubt he'd wish to participate in Mr Houdini's show."

Beck shook his head. "Actually, your friend is about the only famous man in the world who I'd keep off a stage with Harry. Houdini's in the habit of getting Police Chiefs and Lord Mayors and what-have-you to search him before he gets locked up, to prove he's not made any preparations to cheat his captivity. I don't think it'd be smart to ask Sherlock Holmes to do that, do you?"

I chuckled at the thought. "Probably not."

"Just call in and enjoy the show if you can. We'll be debuting a new trap. I can't say what, yet, but its good. And we'll be doing one of Houdini's big set piece challenges two days before, a stunt at Tower Bridge next Saturday. It'll be big."

"I can't make any promises. Holmes has a new case which is drawing all of our attention."

"And he doesn't want any distractions, right? Obsessive about getting every detail nailed down and shining a light into every shady corner? Yeah, I've been there. Still, if you do drag him out to the show make sure you call backstage before or afterwards. I know Houdini would be pleased as punch to meet you and your pal."